PEARL

NIAMH DOLORES

Pearl by **Niamh Dolores**

Print Edition

My Deepest Love and gratitude
to my beloved Timothy Porter, who gave me the
gift of flight.
And to my sister Eimear who designed the artwork.

Contents

1

A WARM BREEZE

A warm breeze settles on my shoulders like a shawl,
I feel you.

ONCE UPON A time ago, where time is not, two starlights of crystalline beauty basked in luminescence until their numinous auras met a dark haze, completely shrouding their light. That meeting caused their descent.

At that exact moment, on Earth time, at the ripened age of sixteen years, Pearl had her first brief encounter with Rocks. He sat beside her on a train on London's underground tube. Neither one acknowledged the other only Pearl experienced a strange occurrence. She had blacked out for what seemed an eternity, and just as a star fallout the night sky – it was all of a seconds flash. Rocks left the train, and destiny aligned their meeting once again. Not until some years after. In a nightclub, on her 19th birthday, this time, he noticed her. It was the silky little black number, dress-like liquid on her skin.

He blocked her with his foot. He had not anticipated she would trip. What did I do that for, he thought? He couldn't help himself regardless of his move that went unnoticed. He was good at that. But Pearl, floored, knocked her head on the ground.

Her concussion lasted moments, yet she found time-lessness in that realm. In which a warming breeze held and elevated her. The noise of chatter and music muffled, almost silenced in the background as she distanced, floated, then entered an expansive brilliant blue. Just blue. Everywhere, where she heard the faintest whispers:

"Pearl. It is time to return to the dark promise of restoration and remembrance."

1

THE DRIVE & IN-BETWEEN

Did I get taller or
is the sky today lower?
The moon, the sun…
everything seems closer.

6 years later.

OH, SHE DOES. Pearl has suspicions alright but cannot see through a canopy of thick fog.

Typical English weather, she thinks when strange as it seems, a warming breeze settles all about her, prompting her to look up only to see a perfectly blue hole in the sky. *If I look through a certain angle and tilt my head* – as though bending her vision – *I can see beyond the upper layers of cloud.* She gasps. Her mind silences, and her eyes, breathless, reflect the orangy-red disc floating in the sky when a giant, bulbous cloud appears. An entire archive of silvery-white architects itself, towering up and down and all around, encircling her.

She is on the edge of in-between worlds – blue sky, total blackness, two stars. Places she transports to after feeling a warm breeze on her skin.

There's something alive in the air, these banks of cloud, she senses, *filled with stories over time.*

Little does she know what they know and hold. As the clouds move by, there is a sudden flash of brightness as they let in the sun. *Am I really up here?* Squinting, she turns away. And then she is not. She is grounded in the City of London. Waiting for Rocks to pick her up, he is late, she watches city robots come and go…

In circles, off to work, back and forth, over and over, dreams duplicated the whole day round, like rolls of film, over and over again.

Where are we all going? she thinks.

Day in, day out, year after year after year, appointments, meetings, in and out of slots, back to back, everything neatly fitted. Deadlines, tensions, pressures, moulding you, distracting you, creating an obsession with the linear of time. Endlessly, trying to get somewhere, to be someone.

For what exactly, rushing towards what? She thinks.

Pearl sighs, her mouth opening slightly as she embraces the vision. Those circuitry thoughts started a mild paranoia, that over the years, grandfather clock turned time itself into an entity; of a full-blown presence conspiring against all of human race, gravitating towards time.

Time…

How time consumes all in everyday doings, wearing

out the skin, robbing each one of their nature and humanness. Connected to bleeping phones harnessed to bodies, as though an extension or upgrade of themselves-turned-computers, appearing human-talking screens, streams of notifications, explosive alarm clocks blasting nerves, and all beeping, rushing, to go where?

Pearl laughs at the thought of the invention of clocks, how Man created that pressure for himself by the conditioning of time. A classic backfire.

What a beauty in nature's twist she thinks. Despite taking extreme measures to avoid that existence, she always found herself caught up in it, thinking about it. It made her smile, the ever-looming tick-tock, tick-tock… when Rocks drives up beside her.

Oh, a brand-new Mercedes? she thinks.

"A'right?" Peering through the black window screen as it slides down.

"Er, whose car is this?" She knows it's not his.

"Get in," he insists, "we're going for a drive."

She walks around the back and up the left side of the car, and enters the front passenger seat of the two-seater. As soon as she shuts herself inside the car, Rocks rams his foot on the accelerator and attacks a sleeping policeman. The car floor claps, the suspension wails and her blood screeches coldly through her body.

"Wh… are you deliberately trying to destroy this car and *whose* is it?"

"Pffff… the geeza owes me money so I'm borrowin'

his mota."

"Right," Pearl hesitates. "You're abusing a perfectly fine car. What's wrong with yours?"

"Don't wanna abuse a perfectly fine car, do I?"

She looks out of the window, at life passing by. Pushing through London's clogged arterial roads. As part of that congestion, they head north of London.

"Look at that sky," she says, tilting her head back in awe. The very sight of eternity itself glowing beyond the cloud cover – *the greatest lie of the sky.* It could have been any other day of Englands grey tear-filled clouds pressing down on Earth, but not today. The blazing sun quickly forces an open sky, and reveals an uplifting blue without a trace of yesterday's winter. She looks up again; something about the grand spray of light that shines out from the cold black of space touching billions of tiny pores, millions of miles below. Its darkness penetrating promises of sun-drunken smiles, that life again is good – removing the thrash of memories drawn from the harsh elements of a long and bitterly cold winter.

Apart from Rocks, whose agitation makes an unforeseen turn into London Gateway services.

"You okay?" she asks him.

"Yeah, I just…" his throat dries up as he steers into the car park. He wrenches the handbrake.

Stop.

Rocks is in his thirties, and always has a woman by his side. Raised by his gambling father while taking care of his mother, he learned that by keeping her weak she would never leave. His childhood consisted of countless evictions and repossessions – many times over – moving from mansions to bedsits, riches to rags. As a repercussion of that gain and loss, possession has become of primary importance to Rocks. It makes him rush. And Pearl is his weakest spot; she excites him. As well as money.

He looks at the key in the ignition, hesitates, then looks into Pearl's eyes. He composes himself.

"Get some juice, shall we?"

She dismounts from the car beset by suspicion. Fixing her feet steadily on the ground, she braces herself. Brushing her thighs in one, two downward sweeps, brushing her nerves onto her jeans.

"Here, hold this," he says, thrusting a white plastic bag in her hand. "Gotta run to the…" He whistles a high-low melody through pursed lips, his eyebrows lifting and falling in sync.

As he makes distance, he turns to look back at Pearl with that look in his eyes. Do not move. His masterful tone is one she obeys. She stands there holding the white plastic bag beneath the blue sky. When a great cloud rolls in. It elongates and spans like the yawning wings of a swan's flap before spanning a smooth glide, veiling the blue. As though the blue itself takes off, Pearl to wants to flee. She senses something is not right but stands firm beneath the shadow of the cloud while Rocks chases his feet into a busy shopping centre. Within seconds, he is out of sight.

What is he up to? she thinks as he leaves her standing centre of a human storm. Amid the chaotic whirl, Pearl recalls some years back. Not long after her 19th birthday. She stood outside a derelict warehouse in East London. Rocks kept her waiting then, too. Alone in the night... with the wind, having nothing to recollect but its own fury, tossing the air. She didn't see the forewarning of wrath, raptured in swirls of its balletic display, when a gust slapped her across the face.

Reality check.

You stupid girl, she thought. That she subjected herself to such dangerous conditions, out there in the thick of night.

"Who's there?" Her scattering eyes searched. Who *was* there but falling shadows, smothering her enquiry. Who would hear her desperate wasteland cries? Would the wind drift and carry her pleas, and who would hear? Her calls echoed and stayed alive for miles until their dissolution met with a vast emptiness – at least that's what Pearl thought but such calls are never unheard, never forgotten, never unknown. A part of her communed with that rich blackness:

Save me from drowning in this deep sea of night, she pleaded. Weathered, inside and out, she longed for the wind take her to some faraway planet. And in her nostalgia to float away, a subtle warmth filled her senses.

Pearl lifted and floated – neither in nor on the gravity field of Earth, or any named location.

What's happening… I'm floating, drifting, I can't feel the ground… Just total blackness. *Stop!*

When a tickling above her crown transported her back, she stumbled and felt a warm hand touch, as if someone, or something, had prevented her fall.

What was that, is someone here? she thinks.

"Oh! You sweet thing –" it's a ladybird. "– what are you doing here all by your little self?" Fluttering above her head, steadily, into the wind, it's as if the ladybird warned she stay away. Pearl almost sensed a reply but was distracted by the chill of darkness that burrowed through her body. She looked for shelter and spotted a derelict theatre. One foot before the next followed the shadows that brought her closer towards whats left of the broken structure. Its crumbling loom reflected her mood, for she was weak, and the wind swirled, wrapping its tentacles around her ankles reaching its portal, and claimed territory within her hollow empty tin.

If this Rocks guy doesn't turn up soon, I will die here, waiting, she thought, as the sound of a prowling car resembling a suspicious cat approached. She listened as the rubber wheels depressed the gravel, and deflected those turbulent thoughts weft by the wind.

Then, "For goodness sake," she moaned, stunned by the glare of headlights. She squinted and shunned the superior lights that like a double star lit the night of her mind. Its brightness triggered an orbit within, and at the same time, a warm breeze.

Oh God, it's happening again.

Suddenly, she returned to that blackness but spun like a Catherine wheel, between sun and moon, dark to light to dark she waned like a speck in the great black of space. Ever-increasing and decreasing in a circuitry loop until her orbit distanced to the furthest point of total darkness. Unlike the darkness of shadows, this a richer blackness, one of deep-vast-space. A refuge she had not yet recognised. And there it was, that same warm gentle hand touch just as moments before. A presence, curious and shy. Only this time, a bedazzlement of merging lights trailed her periphery in circular white-gold mist.

Oh God, please go.

Feared by this mysterious unknown that seemed to touch, she slipped back into her physical body when a tall figure shadowed the entrance of where she stood. And finally, face to face, Pearl met Rocks.

His mood couldn't wait to intimidate her.

"Wot's your name?"

"Pearl," said with an appeasing smile.

He hesitated and became guarded by a sudden thought that he'd been followed or set-up. His shifty gaze turned left then swiftly right over his shoulders. His quiff flopped, hiding his ice-blue eyes behind rich strands of black hair.

"Who sent you 'ere, where d'ya live?"

"I... ahem –" (she was wary) "– live in the City, West End."

"Ah. Rich girl." He paused. "Ow d'ya get out 'ere, someone drop ya off?"

The pellets of his questions bombarded Pearl – she could tell he was troubled. His intense stares awaited a reply that burst forth an awkward silence and held them in utter stillness. Unable to utter a word beneath the mercy of his frosty reception, she thought he would top her up and, wahey, off she would go.

No.

It didn't work like that.

♦

THE SCRUTINY OF his eyes penetrated the entirety of her body. Head to toe. Scanned for clues, regardless, one way or another, he was bound to the eventual weakness that predicted his fall – and so his tone softened, almost to a whisper.

"How can I trust ya?" he said, sinking into her mill-pool eyes when, *bam*. The desperation in her pierced him. He recognised her desire only too well, even a second's glance to someone 'without' is too raw to bear. The resistance too great. He wanted to cave in. It angered him greatly that she mirrored him back to *that* place. He fidgeted, moved his hands inside his jacket pockets. Carefully held a pre-rolled joint in one, a Zippo in the other. The intent touch of his rough skin on smooth paper and metal calmed the edge of his quick-to-crack mood. He placed the joint between his lips and flipped open his Zippo. The smell of leaking gas turned her stomach. The sound of grinding metal grated her skin.

He fired the end of his twisted joint. It burned her eyes, drawing on the brilliant orangey-red embers like that. And in one flick, he closed the fusion Scorpio brass lid. Pearl's eyes fell on his swollen, tattooed hands. She began to fade as an alarming, growing red filled her vision. A warning sign she noticed, and dismissed.

His lungs clung onto the sedative fumes, which permeated his insides, then he blew out a parched breath:

"Ow long you been usin'?"

If there was a positive side to her desire it was that it came with fierce valour – she continued piercing her gaze through his, and sure enough he melted, and dropped all defence.

"Sorry, ya know, ya got me scared," he confessed. "Thought I was gonna get busted again." He thought she was an undercover cop. "Just got out of prison, tryna turn a new leaf, 'en I." He spoke with sincerity.

Yeah, right.

As if hearing her thoughts, he said, "Na. Seriously, I'm finished with all this. I'm clean now. Gonna start a new life."

Pearl's eyes enraged with flames. The surge of anger and disappointment fuelled her weak body. She wasn't interested in hearing how clean he was, how he was about to start a new life just as she was about to dirty hers. Justifying himself like that only emphasised the opposite worlds they came from. She didn't want to be separate from what she set out to do. Nevertheless, she struck the bad in him, and like a match her fire caught at him, aroused his old ways. God help her, that he stood alone with this pretty young thing, vulnerable and far from civilisation. And knowing her weakness, the realisation of which made him smile a wicked, deceiving, rotten smile. A smile that seduces and exploits all that is good.

"As angry as Scarlett," he teased. His perverse sneer seeped into her pores and lingered within her crumbling structures.

"Who, what did you say?"

"You're actually irresistible when you're angry," he said, palming her delicate jawline, "way too beautiful for this junk..." Oh, what I could do to you, he thought.

Have we met before? she thought. She couldn't be sure. She looked at him, properly. His body shape firmly complimented his clothes. She looked away shyly, then flickered her eyes in all directions, yet secretly enjoyed his intimidating stares. He took a step closer, backed her against a wall. Her fear excited him, provoked his move even closer. She felt the warming air from his nostrils, and the nakedness of her raw lips quivered beneath the threat of his. His scent imbued her as his lustful smile wandered all about her fragility. Oh, how she yearned for his destruction. You see, these are dangerous moments for someone in ruins.

♦

ROCKS THE POSSESSOR revelled in such opportunities as these, but maybe he *had* changed.

"You shouldn't be alone," he said. "Not 'ere." They exchanged valuables: his potent warmth for her pricey paper.

"Wait," she remembered. "It *is* you. You helped me a couple of weeks back."

He looked at her blankly.

"In that club. You hung out with me to make sure I was alright."

Still nothing but both smile broadly.

"I tripped."

"Ah…" The ever opportunist couldn't believe his luck. "Well, well…"

"What happened, you disappeared?" she asked.

He turned quiet. Then,

"You shouldn't be 'ere alone," he winked, backing away.

Maybe he had turned a new leaf after all.

"Don't let me see you again," his wanting smile warned. He absconded and left her wondering if he would.

Why has he turned like that? She thought, but as

soon as the opiate warmth filled the palm of her hand, potentiating, sensitising her, sheer relief impregnated every cell of her being. For now, he had become non-apparent, and so had the urban wasteland as it opened a brilliant passage of poppies meandering like a velvet orangey-red river. Either side, tall golden reeds swayed generously in the wind; they swished open an invisible tube, and Pearl passed through. Touched by that shimmering golden warmth, her body hosted shuddering energy that shot up from the ground.

This feels familiar.

Electrical currents of spine-tingling nerves laddered up her nape into a shivering crown. Twinkling sensations popped every follicle alive like phosphorous, illuminating hundreds of thousands of neurons, separating skin from cloth. Her pores, magnified, erected into wakefulness, and as time sped dark into day. She gasped at the emerging sun turning the whole sky red. Its brilliance glistened the early hours below, where droplets of dew blanketed the breathing earth like the surface of shimming water. Pearl smiled at her liquid face reflected below, stunned.

I'm here again, I can touch the sky, and it's so warming. Her endorphins lifted and stretched more. *Am I really up here?* She switched into sudden darkness. *This is wild, floating in black space...* with the same gentle hand-touch trailing misty white-gold lights, just like before, only the lights morphed into lyrical melodies and swathed her in utter beauty. Peace and tranquility. *What's touching me… its harmonising, so pure and soothing… Hello…?*

Her quests swallowed by emptiness were not unheard and she received a responsive sound that faded in and out. A lower frequency entered one ear, a higher resounded in the other.

What is that? The sounds vibrated inside of her. *Wait… A pair! Two!*

And again… as if to caress her. "Who's doing that?" She spoke aloud.

Oh! My eyes, my scalp, it's… lifting off, I feel headless and light! Then, she shifts again. *Blue?*

Blue. Just blue. Everywhere. Shimmering all around. She stretches into endless blue, floating, devoid of All thought. Sensing something alive in the air – its omnipresence sitting timelessly here, there, before, after, above, and below. Its distance an immeasurable, speechless blue. But a stark edge of brilliant white cloud appears when a clumsy man bumps into her at the service station, *oomf,* brushing her past away in one sweep.

Recovering from the knock, Pearl looks at the white plastic bag sitting on the ground.

"Oh no!"

Much quicker than she, the man picks up the white plastic bag placing it back in her hands.

"Here, I'm so sorry," he said, "are you okay?" his gentle eyes comfort her.

"No, I'm sorry," – (pauses) – "I'm fine." She insists. Looking up, she stares vacantly – "I…" – then looks down to the ground – "…was miles away."

She hears: "The treasure of truth is above the sky."

She looks back at the bag in her hands, noticing its significant difference in weight. By the time she returns her gaze, he has disappeared. And Pearl is lit by the remarkable déjà vu exchange of unspoken action through hands.

♦

SUDDENLY, ROCKS STANDS before her.

"Ah. The wanderer returns," she says scornfully, happy to see him, relieved and resentful all at once.

Swiping the white plastic bag from her, he asks, "Is that s'pose to be funny?"

She doesn't care, indulges in the freedom pouring though her empty hands. That pouring is a quench, equalling a naked-leap into fresh waters until the next moment charges her back in sticky air – something does not feel right – as he places the car keys in her hands.

"Wait," he says, under his breath. "In the car."

She knows better than to challenge him, and it isn't long before he joins her in the car. He fires the engine and exits the service station. Sliding down the slip road back onto the motorway, there's a transitory blur; it's the slow-drive alongside whizzing traffic that gives a sense of squashing time. Pearl's lucid eyes watch the service station shrinking in the wing-mirror, where she sees a figure holding the white plastic bag. That's me, she thinks, touches her lips and looks at her fingertips, but I'm not wearing lipstick.

The reflection of her arrest by undercover police plays out, but the scene reduces rapidly to the size of a vanishing-dot in the wing-mirror as Rocks accelerates to full speed. He merges with the motorway, catching up with time.

Then turns to Rocks, whose moist forehead turns out beads of sweat that drip down his temple, then his cheekbone. His quiet relish in victory is much louder than he cares to realise. Unaware of the seeping smile from the back of his rotting head to the outer corners of his mouth. That smile. How could he. And how could she, how could she want a smile that reeked of violation. Studying his animated, magnified pores, she has never seen him so ignited.

She stares directly through the windscreen. The sun-lit sky dims as a cloud arc closes in on the horizon, like an eyelid. Pearl rests behind her eyes where inner worlds rise and fall. It makes sense to her now why he'd used someone else's car and not his. Sickened by his deception:

He's got fucking mud all over his face, she thinks.

She has to ask.

"Rocks. What is in the bag?"

2

SILK COCOON

Over the wide darkness,
floating freely.

PEARL AND ROCKS reach the end of the M1 South, when her pent-up rage reaches its peak. They're about to pass through an intersection of traffic lights as the red-amber-green sequence flashes *GO*. As if the signal gives her permission to flee, she leaps in a second's opportune. Rocks, forced to flow with the traffic onto the North Circular, is seething, hitting the steering wheel, that she escaped him.

"She is gonna pay for that."

Pearl bolts towards Brent Cross bus station, red-faced and wheezing, boards the 189 new Routemaster, and the doors swiftly snap behind her. Unlike the convenient old-style hop-on-and-off London buses, she thinks, exhausted but relieved that she can now journey home safe from Rocks.

But not for long. A few stops ahead he suddenly appears on the bus from nowhere, pounding towards her like a wild beast. The next moment he's yanking her hair hard, dragging her down the aisle. Her eyes plead as she is pulled to the back of the bus, passing seated commuters who drop their heads into phones like invisible plugs.

Why aren't you helping? People, please! she silently begs. He is raging. No one wants to help. He props Pearl up on the back seat, squashing the side of her face against a window.

"You're hurting me," she squeals. Closing her eyes, she turns inward as though entering deep silence. *Please help me.*

The bus driver, watching the commotion in the mirror, brings his bus to a standstill. And as though transforming his small, unnoticed body into an equally raging roar down the aisle:

"Get – off – my – bus."

Now, even though the driver's threat guarantees a savage consequence, there comes about a strange healing energy that pours into Rocks. Softening him, he smiles. He lets go of Pearl and walks off the bus leaving everyone to sit with their mouths open, speechless and stunned by his miraculous, unexplained change of mind. Including Rocks, he does not know what changed him.

LATER, REACHING THE last stop Pearl thanks the bus driver with a smile and walks the back streets from Marble Arch to her Soho flat, still shaken.

Please don't turn up at my house, she thinks, as her

reluctant footsteps speed to a panicked run. Reaching the front door she clumsily inserts the key, fumbling for what seems an eternity, the door opens then her feet fumble up the climb of stairs until finally, she is indoors. Home, a safe place where freedom awaits behind closed doors. Folded... packed... sealed inside, alone in a box. A finality that marks either the end of a day, or completion of one's physical life, where insignificant problems melt away.

Pearl removes constrictive clothing from her body, making her jeans, undies and jumper redundant, squashing the material on the ground with her feet. She stands naked, grabs a dressing gown then makes her way through to the living room. She's on the edge of elegant collapse and draws the curtains, shunning the midday light for introversion as the black moon rebounds for a shining sky to recede. Then ritual has its way; a purge before hibernation. She builds a smouldering fire then sparks all the candles alive with the lighter. The flickering threads of fire strewn along the mantelpiece switches on her shadow, dragons tower the walls around her. She inhales. Enters the opiate world. No longer desperate to forget what happened at the service station earlier, she exhales a sprawl over the sofa, indulgently sipping the smoke-filled air. A mind cleanse from the city dirty-human humdrum, no longer riding mundane thought that masquerades through every pore, no. She exchanges this for the seduction of empty black space. Sinking deeper into the sofa, she is wrapped in silvery veils, a liquid state, when she hears a colony of seagulls pass over.

Seagulls… She smiles.

She slips into momentary silences, before and after the sound of squawks, moving in and out of silent air transports. As though the echoes of their calls lures her far away with them, drifting into the vast horizon – where the sky becomes water.

I'm swaying side to side.

A subtle swish, in and out of stillness like a creaky boat wanders about the open sea. How she longs to slip, as an oar lets go and sinks into the ocean's depth. She, too, wants to go, unnoticed, to merge with spirit. To let go of worldly chaos and destruction, and leave it to continue the undoing of itself. Unlike the flocks of society, tarnished by its oil-slicked wings hindering its transmutable flightpath to Utopia. She ponders on the gulls, how they settle inland to the nearest out-of-sight rooftop or pasture-resembling patch of wilderness for another night's survival. Wondering…

Is my navigation any different from the gulls? Am I just surviving? There's more to life than just existing, I just know, I feel it…

The figure-like shadows cast by the light of the candle-flames encircles Pearl, and into that a presence appears. It would seem she somewhat wills the dark, but this has a Grandmother air to it, full of silent wisdom, and with a quiet confidence that needs smile only few words:

"You will see."

Wait, that's not a shadow, Pearl thinks as it hauls itself through the thick red carpet-pile with a stop-start motion.

She expels a great sigh of frustration. "Can I not be alone, anywhere, without interruption?" And that it should be so bold as not only to enter *her* space, but to sit right beside her! "Of all the places you can nestle or scramble to, why here now, next to me?" Another sigh. I wouldn't mind but it's a bloody tank, she thinks. Confronted by the black, chunky specimen of a spider she utters more unfriendly tuts and sighs. Only this time, louder. Maybe it will take the hint of her disapproval. But beside this psychodrama she sits with bewilderment; that her fears have vanished. If this were any other time, she would have reposition the spider somewhere, anywhere. Outside perhaps. As long as it's tucked away, out of sight! No. She lets the spider sit beside her, as if to listen to what it might have to say.

"Look, as long as you don't get any closer… you can stay," she tells the spider. Just then a fresh chill blows through the air; she shivers, and exactly as a smouldering fire sparks a flame, a bright golden flash lights up the room, and an explosive velocity thrusts her forward.

It's a brutal smack that shoots hard up her spine then down her arms. Her bellows crack open the night sky, where wefts of written cries tear open what tissue and fascia hold her together. And then the living room floor suddenly drops, and she rises. She can see herself lying on the ground below.

"What's happening?" she mumbles, rippled, in and out of pain and bliss, and fear and dreaminess. She jerks and quivers before paralysis spreads like a drop of ink blackens clear water, obliterating all feeling. Pearl lies shattered beside the spider's delicate and limp body. A teardrop, just one, luminous like silk, shimmers from the corner of her eye and leaps off her cheek in a silken line. She looks directly into the spider's eyes which are staring into hers. You see, deep down inside, she knows.

Oh spider, dear. An eternal longing is pouring from inside of her. *You feel my fear, my pain and entrapment, and at the same time an overwhelming love. I know you do, and it's a great, enormous comfort to me.*

In an ordinary physical world, looking down at herself on the ground like that, she would be filled with questions: What am I doing down there when I'm up here? How am I in two places at once? And she would beckon in fear, Pearl! Wake up! But she doesn't. She can't bring a thought to life, and she tries. Oh, she tries, searching archives of data and genetic information to stream back into her physical consciousness, but every last word disappears without a trace.

Pearl has entered a state of no-identity that pushes even the last rise and fall of thoughts away. It would seem both souls, Pearl and the wise spider, have merged, leaving behind their lifeless shells. She cannot fathom how the silvery lines snapped and unwrapped, voiding the linear web that wires her to her ancestors, instead she accelerates beyond the black moon night into boundless space. No longer entangled by the web of mundane life, but beyond locality and before causality, home, towards nirvana. And in that darkness, floating freely in pure presence, a radiance shines through her entirety, and she shimmers like a pulse.

♦

Later that day

THE SKY IS grey like slate, merging with the concrete ground, no nature, no trees nor the sweet company of birdsong, no elements, at all.

Emerging from the sweeping grey stands a girl. She holds a white plastic bag.

"I'm waiting for you." She softly beckons, reaching out a hand.

"I'm here," Pearl replies, when an enormous crash wakes her from her comatose sleep in the bedroom of her flat. "What, was that a crash?" Her body thrusts up in fright. It's the slam of the front door shaking the porch downstairs. She hears footsteps. Thud, thud, thud, climbing their way up inside the Victorian conversion, Pearl is at the top. Her eyes stretch wide, ironing out her frazzled optic nerves. There are three taps on the front door of her flat.

Oh no, that sounds like his knock. Not now, she thinks.

She doesn't want to see Rocks, not after he tricked her earlier at the service station. Too weak to spend her anger, she lies horizontal, her hazy double-vision wishing him away, when the turn of a key opens her front door.

"He has a key?" She mutters.

She feels a clammy response from the ravine of her core yet parched by the lack of life-force within her structural avenues. And beneath the power of a throbbing head-rush, her body paralyses. She shuts down. Wades inside a murky head, using careful breaths of invisible loops in-and-out until the inevitable self-hypnosis transcends her calm back to sleep.

◆

Some hours later...

AS PEARL DRIFTS in and out of dream and sleep, tapping and shuffling noises wake her. That and the warming, brilliant sun-rays streaming through the curtain gap. Two orange-gold strobes, as bold as they like, burnish the wooden floor amber. Stardust particles swirl a whirling dance fantastically inside the two beams. And while the whole bedroom gives off aliveness, her hooded eyes gravitate towards the black, sooty centre of the fireplace. Unused, dead as night, if not for the dim twinkle of fairy lights. Pearl, like the dead embers, is without the light of breath. Unawares of the shimmering space around her darkness.

Amid the cosmic mist the entire flat vibrates.

"What, was that a crash?" She sits up, hearing the footsteps, thud, thud, thud.

She counts three sets of twelve thuds, then a six-second silence – muted by the carpeted hallway. She calculates time and length of each footstep, which takes away the lowly, heavy-head feeling, until she hears again, three taps on the front door of her flat.

"It's me, I'm coming in," Rocks announces and at the turn of a key, lets himself in.

But you're already in, she thinks.

His shadow stands still in the hallway.

"Pearl?" tapping her bedroom door, "can I come in?"

"Erm, yeah, but you're here already?" She is flustered and terribly fraught.

"What are you talkin' about? I've just this second walked in," he claims, standing at the door of her bedroom.

"You've got my house key?"

"Yeah, you gave it to me."

"I did?"

Oh, she thinks, I don't remember. "I thought I heard you come in already?"

He sighs. "Nope." He knows she's wasted. He plays on her confusion: "You must 'ave imagined, or dreamt it." He makes no effort to disguise his disapproval.

I hate him seeing me like this, she thinks looking to her dressing table, laden with chunks of crystal. An opened seventies keepsake jewellery box, and inside, a ballerina. Her arms reach up; she too is without life. Dependent, she waits – stuck in time – it could be months, years before her next short-lived, unwinding dance. Scattered on the floor, junk and empty bottles lie.

"Don't be ashamed." He kiss her on the cheek. Now she gives him a disproving look.

"I'm not, you just gave me a fright, it sounded like you pulled the house down." She hushes him. "You'll wake everyone coming through the doors like that."

She doesn't realise the time, he thinks.

"Well, it's an old 'ouse." He smiles. "Did I shake the walls?"

"The walls? The entire cosmos shook!"

"Sorry 'bout that, nice to see ya smile, though," he says, stroking her hair. "I got us dinner."

"Dinner?"

"Yeah, Pearl, it's tea-time, see?" He opens the curtains.

She peers from beneath the covers, and squints. Even the soft sundown burns her sensitive eyes.

"Oh. I see." The gentle sway of velvet trees like coral on the ocean's bed. "The day *has* gone."

"Oh well, what's done is done."

Done? What's done? she thinks.

Neither one mentions the incident at the service

station earlier that day.

"Let's eat, I'm starvin."

"Oh, while I remember, I've got mice. I can hear their constant shuffling and tapping noises."

"You're imaginin' it. Come on, get up, woman."

"No, seriously, Rocks, the walls are alive."

"Up! That's an order."

She looks at Rocks, he stands, staring.

"Get out my room then," she says, clinging the duvet to her body.

"Course." He winks, closing the door behind. That wink makes her cringe.

Pearl rummages through her clothes on the back of the chair. She selects the same grey, fraying dress she wears day in, day out. This will do, she thinks. Clumsily she pokes her head and hands through all four holes, bottom to top, then sides. Stretching her nostalgic arms in search of the shimmering blue as the surplus material drops down her fragile body. It touches her toes when lots of tiny creatures take flight.

"Ladybirds!" She smiles. There are at least a dozen of them. "So many Ladybirds everywhere, what are they doing…" she wonders in awe.

If she looked closer, she would see them gathering her dress and tugging at it – as if to warn her.

But,

"Pearl?" she is distracted by his call.

"What?" she snaps as his demands draw her into the kitchen.

"Somefin' I made earlier," he winks in jest.

"Is that it? I thought it was something urgent! Did you bring wine?" she asks, impatiently.

"Got a strong kick to it, but the coconut and honey fusion mellows it out," he replies, ignoring her question, playing with her needs. "An o' course, m'special, secret ingredients." He jokes, although Rocks is quite the maestro with combinations. It comes with a critical understanding of precise measurement and timing.

"You look pretty." He smiles.

A great gust stirs suspicion in the sky while the hot sunset turns dramatic blue-black. "Wow," she deflects, looking through the kitchen window. "Such a radical change, looks like we're in for a summer storm. Anyway, you could have cooked here, Rocks."

"Voilà!" To her surprise, he pushes a cheese chunk through her lips.

"Mmm," devouring it. "Tastes good." She smiles.

"Come on." He takes their plates into the living room. She follows. He sits on the huge sofa. It's humid. She opens the French doors, dressed pretty with flower boxes. Geraniums, red, and one pink wild rose. Then she sits beside Rocks, a cushion in between them. They face the sun's lavender-pink afterglow. A mixture of sweet scents wanders through the anticipating warm air. The wind whistles. In response, blustery trees shake like the sound of maracas. Pearl's melancholy stares grasp a pink petal as it clings to its stem. She seems taken by it as though all else cease. The next gust claps the French doors shut, and Pearl watches as the pink petal blows away. Taken by the wind. It blows west, a few miles ahead of night where inky clouds sneak up on the fire, smothered by cyclic patterns scheduled in time – black sun penetrates her mildewed eyes.

"Shall we?" he prompts.

Pearl studies his successive mouthfuls as she shifts her food around the plate.

"Have mine, I'm not that hungry," she says.

"Eat, you need your greens." She eats a little. "Here," he smiles, "your wine," and pours Malbec into her glass. She is caught off guard, pulled into the well of weakness.

"You're always there for me, Rocks, taking care of me while I hide from the world."

"Is that the same Rocks you ran from earlier?" he provokes her, casually. "S'okay, just eat your food."

"I do appreciate you." Uninhibited, she sprawls over the carpet, and her smiling eyes lift and broaden her face.

"That's what friends do, no?" He passes her the big cushion from the sofa. Pawned by his comforts, she leans in.

"Mmm." Her speech slurs. "Like the time you relinquished your fear of spiders to salvage mine!"

"What, the ones who got away?" he laughs loudly, topping up her glass. "Spiders! Arghhh! Two of them on my bed," he mimics.

"Yeah, and I hoovered in the background to make

sure you didn't kill them."

"*Never*, Pearl."

"I know."

"I never saw you move so fast, though. Your reflexes literally propelled you backward like a cat flips its spine... Ha! You screeched like one, too!"

"Great spider-catcher you are! One spun up the wall out of reach, and the other scuttled its legs across the floorboards and disappeared between the cracks!"

"Oh well, outta sight – outta mind," he laughs.

Pearl scrunches her brow. Why do I get the sensation I'm being watched, she thinks. Taking refuge behind closed eyes, she rolls beyond her sockets in endless free-fall. She does not see what the spiders see.

Then, and all the other times she passes out, Rocks helps himself in and around her home. Preparing for the night ahead he washes, cuts some more, and cooks. Then gathers his stashes and leaves for their regular haunt; the Soho Basement Club. You'll wake up at some point, he thinks and kisses her breathless lips. "I'll see y'at the Club, my love." Turning out the lights as he leaves.

Yet he knows – leaving her alone like that is as good as leaving her for dead.

3

MUD UNDERSTOOD

Sometimes the air is violent.
There, there! Shady trees midnight blue,
the air is nonchalantly still.

NOT LONG AFTER Rocks leaves, Pearl survives another binge. This time the phone ringing wakes her.

"I'm downstairs Pearl," a lively voice tells her. "I've been buzzing for ages – can you let me in?"

"Oh… yes, of course. Come up."

Pearl opens the door to Scarlett, her long-time friend, who takes one look at her and says, "Come on," pushing her way in, "I'll look after you," then halts: "Whoah! Looks like a hurricane's hit here."

Pearl's flashback of fragmented wanderings room-to-room in opiate oblivion reminds her.

"I kinda hoped," Pearl explains, "by the time I wake, everything would find its place and miraculously tidy itself up!"

"Oh. You didn't attend the school of Mary Poppins, did you?"

Pearl smiles.

"Don't you worry." Scarlett smiles back, "I'm here now. I'll take care of Everything." Waves her hands as magical wands through the air.

Although, a decade between them, Scarlett's aesthetics does not appear a day over Pearl's. She has a tall, toned physique, and mysterious eyes. Her thick, jet-black wavy hair bounces down the length of her back. She's seen Pearl like this many times before, and so she nurses her, dresses her and paints her face.

"There, there. Like a brand-new shining doll," she smiles. "Ready? I'll fix up the house later, first I need you with me tonight, Pearl." And off they go.

THE PAIR OF them hail a hackney carriage. Driving through the city:

Scarlett chit chats with the driver. "Aren't the roads busy tonight?"

"There's a festival in Hyde Park. Some roads are blocked."

Hare Krishna's chant and dance in the streets.

"Isn't that a strange accent you have?" Scarlett persists. Pearl smiles. "I can hear Scouser, but there is something else?"

"Ah! I lived in Liverpool for four years but I am from Poland."

"What an unusual mix," she replies. "Hey, did you hear that, Pearl, isn't that an unusual mix?"

The carriage fills with giggles. Minutes later, arriving outside one of London's elitist clubs – Antenna Heights, members-only, Scarlett tips the driver, and their click-clack heels make for chatter on their way upstairs to the stunning panoramic views. They sit at a glitzy bar. Scarlett's slender features mirror Pearl's long legs draped over the barstool through the slit of her silvery silk dress.

Looking into each other's eyes, they salute and slam, then knock back amber tequilas. There the night begins. Involuntary shivers take their bodies hostage for some seconds before electromagnetic fields of euphoria spread in a ripple effect. Pearl looks up through the glass dome-shaped roof. The black sky cracks open and reveals a sparkling universe to magnify behind her eyes, and she elevates towards two stars. *The double star, I've seen this before.* She is enchanted as their curiosity encircles her. Pearl then sees herself swimming in the black sea of space, entwined by wefts of silver-gold ethereal threads.

"Uhu…" Scarlett clicks her fingers. "Hello?"

"The night is charmingly endless," Pearl smiles with dreamy eyes.

"The night is young, Pearl." Scarlett says, ominously, as they sit beneath a grand chandelier, its sparkle laden with threat. "Now you're sober, tell me, what did you get up to today?"

More clubbers arrive. A man passing by interrupts them.

"Hi Pearl." Air-kissing her cheeks.

"Hey Darlin'," she ties his criss-cross thread of invisible kisses.

"You look striking, as always."

"I'll catch you later," she smiles with a wink, and continues her conversation with Scarlett. "I was with an old friend, wasting time."

With Rocks, who earned his name by trade. Because he deals in them. Brown ones, white ones, yellow and pink hues... some pure, some dirty, depending on how he washes, cuts and cooks. Pearl doesn't like his name, Rocks. Her inner mind names him Mr Fox.

"I see. And the Ol' boy who said hello," Scarlett asks, "who's that?" She taps her fingers on the bar while Pearl nods her head, both in sync with the music.

"Funny you should ask." Pearl smiles. "That's Dan. Rocks introduced me to him. Years ago."

"Rocks, who you waste time with? I can't keep up with you. How have I not met these 'old friends' of yours... Rocks... Dan...?" She laughs. "Not bad for an Ol' boy! Seems like a real man," Scarlett mocks. "Dan the man."

"I'm sure you know Rocks, Scarlett."

"Oh, I know everyone – but no one knows me unless they are Someone."

A misty cloud ambles through the open patio of the rooftop terrace. Pearl grips the bar as swirls of abstract shapes and flashing lights trail her periphery. Her heart beats inside her knees, lub-dub lub-dub...

Did I ever do you wrong in every way?

A favourite of theirs, *Around* by 'Noir & Haze.' Usually Scarlett and Pearl would leap up in a frenzy and lose themselves in dance. Not now, though, as Pearl contends with the vision of her physical edge. It's blurring. She leans onto the black and gold marbled bar for support. It has a tawny padded leather top.

Ever felt like you've been hurt before, by the ones that said they only loved you more?

"What do you mean, everyone?" she asks Scarlett. "Who's talking about me?"

"Let's get some air." They walk out onto the rooftop terrace. Scarlett picks up from where she left: "Not anymore. Everyone's done talking about you," she replies, rolling her eyes for dramatic effect. As she lights up, her impatience draws on a cigarette, puffing her chest up and out... lungs hold on tight... then imparts with a strained voice: "Do you have any idea how concerned everyone was?"

She channels a train of smoke like a stratus cloud through her red lips. "And who's this Rocks, did *he* leave you in this state? Some friend he is." She tuts.

Inflicted pain and scars of sorrow, like an empty shell I wait for tomorrow.

"The bag, he didn't tell me what was in the white bag."

"You're not making sense, Pearl."

"In the car he picked me up in, earlier, Scarlett. Earlier. In the car. We were heading back into town and I ran from him."

There is no more sun there is only cloudy days…

"You ran, well what did he do?"

"The bag, Scarlett, the white bag. I know it was mindless, irresponsible, running into traffic like that. The timing couldn't have been more perfect – the 189 into town was sitting there waiting when I reached the bus station. Soon as I got on the bus I drifted with the muffling chitchat in the background. People's stories, confessions –" (laughs) "– the secrets commuters reveal on buses. Do you think they realise the whole bus can hear?"

"Buses are noisy," Scarlett smiles. "They're caught out with their raised voices once the bus stops."

"Hmm… Anyway, while people find it easier to open up in public places, listening is my therapy."

Scarlett prompts her: "Back to the story."

"Well," she begins, but then suddenly shouts: "SCARLETT!" as her friend nods off behind a thick plume of smoke. "Scarlett!" Shaking her awake when the cigarette falls on her hand.

"Ouch!" She sloughs off glittering red rock embers. "What are you doing?" Scarlett tuts.

"Never mind me, look at you burning yourself!" Pearl's impish giggles overtake her.

"Go on then, laugh if it makes you feel better about what I said, no harm done," Scarlett retorts.

"Telling me unsavoury stories about the likes of Rocks. No wonder everyone's concerned."

"Who?"

"You think your trembling hands and millpool eyes go unnoticed just because you dress well and epitomise feline elegance. It doesn't disguise that mud, eating your brain." She mops her lips dry with an index finger.

Pearl abandons her impish smile for growing eyes. Wide with concern.

"Truth hurts, doesn't it, Pearl."

Pearl looks over her shoulder; she feels a warm fragrance filling the space around her.

"Who are you looking for, Pearl?" her voice is vengeful, exasperated. "Listen to me." She rummages through her purse for a moment's reprieve, then grabs a lipstick and paints a random stroke of red on Pearl's lips.

"What are you doing, why are you being weird? Why are you angry Scarlett, with me?" Pearl demands. "Do you even know?"

"Oh, come on, Pearl, you think I don't know?" An imperious air projects through her stiffened spine, a suppressed symptom she no longer conceals, looking down on those she administers mud to. "I wish I had your desire to know, Pearl, your longing… for what's 'out-there' beyond all this." She throws her arms through the air. "I've everything and more, too much." Her confession infused with anger makes her body loud, erratic; she stumbles. Impulse leads her to revisit her purse and she moves objects around, absentmindedly. There are clanging tools. A blackened spoon, a lighter… blades, foil. A creamy foundation. She grabs a compact mirror beneath the junk and looks at her lips, painting them red too. Chanel red. Only, the mirror tells of her drugstore fantasies; a Love-Bite Red.

"I hope your angels are not far from you, Scarlett."

Scarlett looks again in the mirror, triggered by the shadows of disappointment time has drawn around her eyes. She snaps the compact shut. "You know, with all my money, I can't even buy what you have. That yearning you have, Pearl, I don't have it. I can't even touch, never mind grasp it. Time has not spared a second's grace on me. I'm just the daughter of a monster who left me to suffer life through his distorted, corrupt views, and that bitch-for-mother-turned-lesbian –" (she laughs bitterly) "– not a surprise, after what he put her through. And you *never* speak of your parents."

Pearl stares coldly at Scarlett. "No. I don't. Do I?" She's sobering up. "Because they are both dead. Aren't they, Scarlett."

"Yes. And it's the only reason we're friends, it's the one thing we have in common, Pearl." Scarlett's growl continues to grow. "But you *never* talk about yours. Were they that perfect that you want to protect me from the waking haunts of mine? Leaving me *his* rage to take back from good souls what he took from me," she says, stabbing her finger into her chest. "And without faith, *your* faith. How could he? How could *he* leave me with something I can't buy my way out of?

"Scarlett, calm down. You're becoming hysterical."

"And YOU? You just waste your faith and replace it with mud." The fiery demeanor climbs within the dome of her ribs. Her fury is colossal. "You're an insult to those lying in the gutter, Pearl. I can't bear you," she spits in disgust. "You make me sick."

Scarlett grabs her fur shawl and swathes her bitter, taut skin, then gathers her bias-cut silver dress.

She stares at Pearl, who is speechless. Kisses her red lips on hers, stretching her hourglass, ghostly body, and drifts out, as if on air, with endless material trailing behind.

Pearl's quiet devastation releases a tear from her eye. Not because of Scarlett's disdain, but of the resurfacing memories she'd worked so hard to push away. She looks around to pursue Scarlett for the hope of resolve but she is gone. Literally, in a puff.

Where did she go, Pearl thinks, glancing at the exit points around the rooms of Antenna Heights. Pearl doesn't see her anywhere but, Ah. She's gone down the glass bubble lift, Pearl decides, and walks towards the sophisticated, futuristic structure. She waves her hand over the sensor. The doors peel open like a satsuma. She enters and it's as though the lift doors sneakily draw in an eerie silence as they shut. She instructs a second wave over the sensor inside, looking down through the chunky glass floor. There are transparent light-shafts beaming through, tipping all sense and balance out of reason. She remembers the tequila shot she had earlier, how strong it must have been.

Oh God help me, I've taken too much.

She composes herself. Fixes her focus on the murmuring voice of the lift – *shoooom*. It's a swift descent, yet she elevates and hangs in space. Floating above an orange blur of city lights, flashing the dead night alive. Her heavy eyes open with fierce alertness as she senses another presence in the lift.

"It is okay Pearl. Keep it together." She hears.

Did the lift stop, is someone here? I didn't hear anyone enter, she thinks. A sudden chill shivers through her – yet the night is stifling hot – as she looks left totally in sync with another, who turns their head right towards her. Staring into each other's eyes, filled with uncertain smiles.

"Are you okay?" The satsuma walls echo.

Distortion mars all sight and sound, a mirroring disturbance of what the other sees. Infinite reflections begin to shape and multiply inside the mirrored lift, bouncing in every direction. As though looking through a kaleidoscope of endless eyes, slipping through fractal worlds, Pearl sees inwardly and outwardly all at once.

Just a the lift doors open, condensation wipes out the thousand facets of herself, polishing her focus. Her red lips remerge from the mirror. Those red lips remind her – she is looking for Scarlett.

Why is she so angry with me? I must find her, she thinks, exiting the lift onto London's night streets as 'Mazzy Star' plays over the tannoy.

Fade into you. I think it's strange you never knew.

She walks through the curved, cobbled lanes of Soho paved by amber lights beneath the night. Swaying through its labyrinth, unaware of the peering shadows that stand rotted behind darkened walls. Black raindrops fall from ashy clouds. She wants to smell the fresh scent of a dewy earth, not the putrid stench of urine that wafts before her. Since her skin is moistened by the rain she cannot help but remove her shoes, and walks barefoot with pattering sounds, relishing in natures musical freshness, when just at the edge of sight a silver flash brings her back on track.

There she is...

Every corner turned Scarlett's trail is like a moving carpet of fireflies. Leading Pearl to...

Oh no, she thinks, she hasn't gone inside the Basement Club has she?

Knowing Rocks will be there, and she does not want to see him.

It's a modest entrance, barely visible. You'd walk straight past it, if not for the throbbing baseline. Its two-second delay reverberates and rewrites the track, *boom, boom, boom*, and her stomach churns. It's not a good feeling. She looks down, notices a luminous pink against the grey concrete slabs pushing back the evident wonder of life. Suppressing all but one stem which pokes through a crack. Though fragile, it boasts a flower. A rose. Its pleasant aroma wafts all about her. Standing outside the club as the rustling leaves gather around her ankles, their hushes move through her body, through empty space. For years she has felt hollow. An empty tin, with rusty bones for pins.

A tramp staggers by her in the street. His drunkenness stands out in the sober air. He wears a camel-coloured coat. It seems to be pure wool, hangs beautifully like silk; only his shoes speaks more accurately about his life, the upper sole parting from the lower like lips. And like a tongue, his sodden socks flap through. That's a nice thing, she thinks. He's with a form of company.

She absorbs his distorted halo as he staggers and sways. Grasping hold of the can filled with thick alcoholic liquid, his body leaning forward; it's the can that holds him up. Blood gushes from his nose, bright and fresh. Now she staggers and sways. Concern for him saddens her, powerless to help. A mother's son, maybe someone's father, she thinks.

"Go inside," he slurs, as blood spurts from his mouth. "Go 'ome, inside."

What *is* he trying to say?

It's as if it's what she needs to hear, standing outside the Basement Club, hesitantly; that she should go inside? But seeing a black bird hovering above, its conflicting shadow takes flight in the opposite direction. This confuses her very much and the wind suddenly drops wherein that stillness, – pure existence knows of the dangers that lay ahead, for the night skies witness the endless unruliness, the rapes and vile attacks. And for the first time Pearl sees herself among the dangers of the underworld, pushers and lowlife users of blackened, tarnished souls. For them, her darkness pins their light.

Not knowing which way to turn, I should be afraid, she thinks, standing in the cold as the wind whistles up a stir. Only an addict would do this, she realises.

"You stupid, stupid girl," the leaves whisper, as though luring her towards her future, they usher her into the cosy, low-roofed underground club of old-stone warm and friendly walls that hug. Full of otherworldly model types, the ratio of women to men low. She looks around, takes in the atmosphere. A clique crowd, she thinks. Scarlett's crowd. Self-important, air-kissing associates of who's with who, or who's had who, filled with gratification and rivalry. It's not for her. Instead, she turns towards the warm array of dark spirited optics: faces of altered promise…

Mmmm… now you're talking. Frangelico, she thinks.

"Let me guess, something sweet… Frangelico perhaps?" she hears, and turns behind to see.

It's a man.

How did he know? She wonders. She wants to tell

him, get lost, but likes his gentle eyes. His demeanour is charming yet humble but with something strange about him. He doesn't fit among this crowd, she thinks.

"Erm, no! Actually. I avoid sweet when I can," she says.

"And that's because you are…"

"Sweet enough?" Both say at the same time, they laugh. Her cautious eyes warm to his smile. She notices how refined he is, his clothes, too. Dressed in the finest of natural fabrics, in creamy and neutral tones. His platinum-blond hair, combed back from his youthful, fresh skin, has a rich wave to it. She notices something odd, though. Hanging over his forearm is a rather heavy coat, a silvery one.

Pearl mutters under her breathe, "he stands out." But no one else notices him – at all.

She then blurts out, "I avoid stimulants that block intuition, you know, sugar… caffeine…" compelled to divulge.

"You are intuitive, no?" He smiles broadly.

Pearl looks back at the barman who, looking back at her, selects a different bottle.

"Ah! Wild Turkey! You changed your mind," the charming man winks.

"Who changed my mind, me or you?"

"Yes, you're intuitively sweet – but he knows you, right?"

"It's his job to know what I want."

"You mean, local phenomena?"

Pearl understands his language. As though switching her on, she reveals, "Tell me, what good are hidden senses to one with addictions to tend to?" She pauses. "You can't perceive anything but the need to feed a craving. First insidious cravings crawl inside, ravish you. Intoxicants, forever leaving its impression, stains the mind like mildew. Despite knowing you don't want what you crave, you still *think* you want it."

"It's the mind's tricks, but when you can't stop for the want of more; it is the very time to stop."

There is a comfortable silence.

"Needs must be fed before you can listen, respond or answer to anyone. Even a loved one," she confides. "With those blinkers on, it takes your attention away from the Whole field. The expansive field of Love."

"Non-local phenomena? Sounds like you know what you are talking about." He smiles.

Her face flashes red. "Sorry. I don't know where that all came from."

"You don't need to excuse your truth, Pearl, never be sorry."

He knows my name, she thinks.

"Suspicion tells me you know yourself more than you realise," he smiles. "Follow your intuition."

"Intuition, suspicion, it all sounds the same." They play in speech with hidden meaning.

"Not suspicious of me, I hope? Now you're paranoid."

"I am?" She is embarrassed.

"A little paranoia is good for you Pearl – keeps you alert," he smiles. "But this energy must be spent correctly. You must tend to this and merge this with the energy of the heart so not to lose sight of what is true. Otherwise, All else of who or what you are not is no different to a hallucinogenic projection."

"I understand. But to merge the energies, you mean, like a conversion?"

"Exactly."

Staring at him she wonders, how?

"Next time you see the ladybirds, step into their energy and you will come to know their messages."

"Sorry, what did you say?"

"It doesn't matter, look, when re-directing the energy of mind, this must only and always be executed via the heart, to purify ones thoughts first, *then* it is fine to step into ones energy field. Along with an *especial* concentration, never claiming *any* energies to be your own."

"The ladybirds?"

"Any ones energy field. Any sentient being. The elements…"

Another comfortable silence.

Especial. She smiles, nodding at his brilliant expression. Acknowledging this not everyday chit-chat, an immense pouring of gratitude upwells from within.

"I know you will understand me when I tell you…"

"Yes, I know," he interrupts, "although you cannot explain how but a part of you recognises me, you feel completely relaxed and realised with me, but you also feel it's much deeper than that. It's as if you are home."

And you know my thoughts? she thinks.

"I know that you can't wait to be alone to indulge in opiates, mud." He smiles. "I know that man Rocks you hang out with does not care for you. And that your friend, Scarlett, is not who you think she is. I know you like to watch your ballerina dance."

Pearl's mouth opens slightly, she's speechless.

"And you are right. I am not of this crowd. Look, I'm Pop. It's good to bump into you again."

She laughs.

"What's so funny?"

"Nothing." She straightens her face.

"You're laughing at my name, aren't you?"

"It tickled me. That's all."

Where have we met before, she thinks, searching her memory, going back in time.

"You should remember. It is not by chance that we met. If it wasn't was for me you'd be…"

"Scarlett!" Pearl interrupts him as the reflection in the mirror behind the bar catches her attention – a sudden strike of silver flashes and dissolves the world around her, including Pop.

"What? Are they…?" sees them in the mirror, "surely not… kissing!" – Scarlett and Rocks.

4

TAKEN

A quiet shell with ears that roar.

PEARL FOLLOWS SCARLETT'S silver trails through the crowd and arrives in a corridor. She stops.

Pop appears beside her.

She is distressed. "Leave me alone." She blurts.

"The treasure of truth is above the sky."

"What?" Her eyes lit but the sudden weight that spread through her body, dim her senses. She makes for the lady's room. She leans on a basin and looks in the mirror. Her pupils are like black pulses, widening then shrinking into microdots. Seeing her reflection, she asks herself: Do Scarlett and Rocks know each other? How? Why would they lie to me? And that man, Pop... who is he?

Nausea torrents around her body, she shivers hot, then cold. Spheres of diamonds fall from her eyes and create multiples of spirals and fragments, chopping and slicing the air around her in a spinning vortex.

Water, I need water... She runs the taps. It's a heavy

gush from the spout. Cupping her hands to break the flow, she splashes her face. The natural downpour of surplus droplets do the impossible by moving against natural laws of gravity – droplets stream up the basin, and up her wet face. Her bones turn to a liquid state.

Oh God! I'm melting…

Stumbling heavy one minute, floating the next, Pearl moves inside a cubicle, closing the door behind. The walls ripple like waves.

The floor, where is the floor…

She tries gripping the bottomless floor by willing her weight into her shoes, clutching for a sense of gravity and balance. She tries to grasp the falling shadows and echoes of background voices. Tries holding onto anything she can, but the raw vibration of music undulates and lifts.

Then slowly her vision begins to reshape. Objects, form. Boundaries reappear and solidify and she sees a cigarette butt lying on the ground. It has red lipstick prints on it.

"Wake up, Pearl," the lips whisper. She breathes through the lips. Her heart pumps wildly, and though unsteady, she at least feels the ground.

She unlocks the cubicle door, and who is standing there but Scarlett.

"Well, well, well. Look at you." Scarlett eyes her up, her authoritative tone governing Pearl. "When did you arrive?" A smile of satisfaction broadens her kooky eyes. "A little in disarray, I must say." Absently powdering her nose, she continues. Heedless of her state, she stuffs her mouth with opiates, mood-enhancing treats. "It's nurse Scarlett here, eat it all up," she mocks, and she pushes it with immense force down her throat. "Don't you dare throw it up."

Swallowing the threats of her promised demise, Pearl's straitjacket-for-skin can't move. Can't fight the substance of Scarlett. "Come on, let's dance." Grabbing her arm, Scarlett chaperones her wildly to an ecstatic dance floor. "I've got you, Pearl."

Yes, you've got me…

The dance floor thumps alive to FeddyB who spins his records like a whirling Sufi. Pearl's suddenly euphoric upturned eyes rapidly lift her mind into a majestic wonderland of smiley faces and happy heads, all bopping inside the sound of one rhythmic beat. Pearl and Scarlett are delirious, laughing in hysterics, so inseparable they intertwine. They are ethereal strands in synchronistic morphing, dancing through the air. They shrink and expand. As a grand mass of starlings seduce a mesmerised sky, their presence overtakes the dance floor and the crowd encircles them until Scarlett breaks away, vaporising their magnitude in a puff. She leaves Pearl to stand inside the tribe, riding the wave of one beat. Without taking her eyes off Scarlett, Pearl watches as Rocks joins her at the bar.

What are they up to? she thinks.

He puts on his jacket, wraps Scarlett's coat around

her shoulders, and they walk towards the club's exit, then through the black veils draping the stone archway. Pearl follows, and stops at the foot of the stairs leading up to the early-hour commuters who brave a shortcut through back-street alleys. She squints as she looks up; it's an ardent sunrise for those with nocturnal eyes.

Once again, she sees Rocks and Scarlett, at the top of the stairs with their backs to Pearl. His arm around her waist. Their bodies sway like ribbons, their hair entwined by the wind upstairs.

I just can't believe what I'm seeing…

Curling into each other like familiar lovers.

Pearl frantically moves up the mirror-walled stairs. She stops beneath shadows of betrayal fallen from cumulonimbus towers. It pains her deeply; her fingers curl into her palms as if to hold herself up while her inner structures collapse. Heart wrenched and devastated, her knees give way, and a blackening takes over her vision as she leans into the mirrors.

The mirrors… they – they're breathing!

The mirror liquifies and pans wide, inhaling Pearl out onto a picturesque mountainside. She stands before a silver mirrored lake, where the birds are chirping and wild flowers bloom beneath a sky of summer clouds. The perfect day, far from her deranged reality, lures her into that flat mirrored lake. The mud squelches between her toes as she wades through still, silky water. Thigh-deep she plunges into clouds and swims through a rippled sky into an expansive ocean of air.

I could stay here forever, gliding peacefully.

But drawn into deeper currents below the water's surface, she hears distant crashes that seem to travel towards her from above.

Thunder?

The thundering drum is alarming. She urges her body buoyant by a subtle swerve, and elevates through a warm patch of underwater sun. When afloat, she basks her face in its radiance.

What is all that noise?

She swishes her legs, and her body follows in a one-eighty degree swirl, only to see a fast and furious crescendo of waves rolling towards her. In her terror, she meets a moment's embrace and faces a huge wall of water before a great gush pounds on her head, thrusting her below. Millions of bubbles twinkle inside her ears. She tries to surface but the bounding waves continue to smash heavily on her chest. She struggles for gulps of hard-hitting air that smack and overwork her frantic lungs. Another wave launches and attacks. Water, everywhere. The forewarning of death suspends time, wherein she finds solace and unfurls, star-shaped, inside a wave, rotating three-sixty degrees.

Rolling contently, motionless, she spins through torrents, swathed in a luminous calm; an impalpable sight through closed eyes. Chaos and turbulence outside yet soft silence inside, there she remains. Like a quiet shell with ears that roar.

♦

IT'S AN ETERNITY but the finite seconds are fleeting, and precipitate her demise. Desperation and will to survive – jeer her into wakefulness, as though looking through glass.

This is so strange, I can see myself, just like before... she remembers the spider: "You will see." She watches as the angry sea pauses, and she pops up from the wave to its surface. Her eyes tilt, and her gaze strolls calmly over the waveless sea. There is an onshore presence permeating the air when suddenly Pearl sees him, standing there. Over there on the shore.

Is that you?

"Rocks? ROCKS." she calls out.

Does he not see me?

"HELP!"

He's looking right through me. Why are you looking through me?

As though a play button turns the waves back into motion, the looming tide of death tirelessly chucks forth.

"HEY," she yells, with all her effort, "Please don't go!" As he disappears. "Don't leave me."

It's not the thought of drowning that has her distraught, her yearning to expand in totality and become full witness with the ocean, which is a place she often frequents, to retreat with the tide. No, not the drowning itself, but no one knowing.

This can't happen, I can't drown alone.

And another wave avalanches. Popping up with nothing to hold onto she clings madly to the ocean's tumult, trying aimlessly in sheer desperation, grasping waves of water. But her hands slip through. Sinking into a once-background drum, she is now inside the oceans beat. Despair ejects from the depths of her belly for a final attempt to retrieve herself from the vanquishing sea.

Help…

A warm breeze carries her muted cries when a gentle whisper answers her pleas.

"Let go, Pearl."

When there is no way out, no choice, letting go is easier, and so Pearl lets herself slip deeper into a peaceful, conclusive depth. And in that, a force of upliftment propels her up and through the water's surface tension. As though an osprey's talons take hold and haul her, she lifts, all the way. Vertically. Grasping the wild air with her lungs. Even the lively butterflies fluttering inside her belly gasp at the sensation of accelerated height…

Soaring. High above.

2

5

INITIATION 2

*Who never forgets but longs
to be remembered…
~ Soul.*

IT'S AS THOUGH the entire ocean freezes below her. Sets of rolling waves suspended in air have formed thousands of ridges in sequential rows and bridge towards the horizon. Its vast surface is like clotted cream; bulbous and fluffy. Varying in colour from fluffy whites, lilac pastels, and candy-floss pinks to light and dark ocean shades of blue. Pearl's eyes stretch with those ridges. Her vision tracks for miles over the Earth's curve towards a huge golden arc. Above that, the sun floats. Its pouring is a decadent liquid-gold pool of sky-scape. Pearl gasps as she realises.

I'm not above the open sea. I'm above an ocean of crystal clouds, shimmering in the blue atmosphere. As though stepping back to take it all in, the Earth, like a ball thrown through the air, distances from Pearl at such great speed. She cannot fathom what is happening.

What?... wait, am I actually in-between Earth and space?

She is in disbelief. Disorientated. Neither in or on the gravity field of Earth, Pearl is all alone, drifting, waning like a microdot into the coldest black of space. She travels to the furthest point of total darkness, then orbits between sun and moon. The sun, a switch, lights up her face before disappearing into thick, black, lonely space. Then again, switch; her face full of moon. She is increasing and decreasing in a circuitry loop when a bedazzlement of merging white-golden lights trail her periphery.

These silver threads... wefting, wefting, wefting around her, *I've seen this before,* as she spins, spins, spins like a Catherine wheel at rapid speed, never stopping. Then suddenly, Pearl halts in perfect stillness. The lights dissolve. Once again, she enters total blackness, and in that, she becomes receptive to the memories of a forgotten mystery. She hears, "It is time to return to the dark promise of restoration and remembrance."

Is that was this is? And those tranquil sounds... I've heard those too... that touch, and hand caress... that vibration...who's there?

Her questions, just as before, are swallowed by emptiness but are not unheard, as silent space – a felt, living presence, responds through Celestial sounds. They are morphing, lyrical melodies that curiously encircle her. They fade in, they fade out. A lower frequency enters one ear, a higher resounds in the other.

My entire face is lifting! Stop! Who is… doing that? My eyes. My scalp! Oh! My scalp is lifting. I feel headless! And light! Exactly as before, the same sequence.

Sensing this presence, she then realises: *Another…?*

Entities… *It's a pair! Two pairs!*

She is unsure exactly how many, because of all the resounding tones.

Are they multiplying sounds, in pairs?

Strangely, by some kind of magnetism, Pearl becomes a sound. Gravitating to and fro as a wave, she emulates it in response. Her skin, flashing, luminous, blinks like phosphorous as the sounds transmit: stimulate, amplify, layer and harmonise in consonance until all frequencies meet simultaneously in ecstatic perfection. She is totally swathed by dulcet tones in a sheer-woven silk, floating in space. Then all of a sudden they unwrap from Pearl, trailing their sounds into the thick, black distance. Luring her like a snake charmer. She drifts on their echoes until they dwindle into silent space.

In their absence, there comes about an utter emptiness. Utter silence. She is again alone in that black space, neither sun or moon, and it's as if space itself pervades from inside her being, blackening from the inside out, beyond her physical outline, until she is without form.

Just when the unfathomable couldn't become any more, the Celestial sounds return, their presence and force much greater than before. If visible, she imagines, they'd be the flare of the Aurora lights whirling their song around her in astounding sync.

What NOW is happening? My body is throbbing.

They amplify commune with Pearl through sensation, a pulse. Then,

"Relax." She hears as the resounding tones turn into a voice, hushing and overlapping. "Shhhh."

"Hello?" Pearl wants to communicate with the formless voices whose angelic choir of singing harps flatter the raucous air.

The ineffable continue to penetrate their sound waves and morph through her body from the inside out.

"What is that… Who's touching me?" she asks out loud, not yet realising they, of course, know her thoughts.

"Don't be afraid," the soothing voices say, and stroke her in a deep motherly, caring way. Hushing her with the most highest ordain she will ever come to know. "Listen."

Pearl, a silver pulse in heavenly delight, floats in space completely and utterly mesmerised, never imagined such an ecstatic pouring of Love. As she listens into that silent darkness she senses,

"Am I about to enter something?" she asks.

They pulse in response then unwrap their octave sounds again, this time giving her Earth body a great push home – *Whoosh* – through the wildest and fiercest of elements.

6

THE VOYAGE BEGINS

Oh sky take the day,
for the night rays and stars
to shine the way.

IT'S A GIVEN breath of life-force. Butterflies reawaken as she torrents through the ionosphere. The G-force – hard hitting – gushes through Pearl's airways. She resists; her body contracts and she becomes unstable. This no easy task; to balance in an anti-gravity field of ferocious air currents.

Tumbling in feverish bellows of stops and starts, spinning in space, she is spared not by echoes of lost breaths and missed heartbeats – clinging to the mortal life she knows.

Where are you?

The warming breeze reappears with a firm but gentle prod, changing her direction. Pearl finds herself floating back in the thick of space, but the Celestial sounds fade as fast as they appear, and their light-trails diminish into blackness.

"Don't go, please, don't leave me."

Whatever you are, don't go.

She tries to will them back, but the dwindling trails cease. Her will is not yet strong enough, and again she descends like a rocket toward the blue planet.

My head, it hurts.

And into the blazing, beautiful blue. Although falling, a moment suspends her in time: High above breathtaking sights of cloud, lilac-tinted cotton-wool. The monumental cloud terrain is dense with groves, contours and tones, illustrating networks of paths and ridges, spreading the scale of continents like a giant-sized map of the sky. She glimpses through sporadic dewy-holes of cloud, at the vivid blue and emerald-green of opal seas below. The earthy rich colours are a pure transparency of the life she once knew. She gasps.

Home.

But for the first time Pearl acknowledges the outline of her body, up there in the sky, and she is panicked, by her body in the air above the shore!

What is this, why am I up here?

She cries out loud at the distance between her toes and Earth below, when an enormous, brilliant silvery-white, huge cauliflower-head appears. The closer it expands towards her, the larger it grows, taking up all of the sky. Her panic rides along its ever-increasing edge.

"Breathe, shhhhh, breathe."

"You're back! Thank God!"

She is swathed in bliss by the subtle, ethereal strokes of super-loving, all-encompassing pulse waves. It's as though she hitches a lift and journeys the cloud's curve all around when a wide-blue opens and pervades from inside her vision. Floating atop an Earth-sized crystal ball, she catches her breath.

This is beautiful.

Blue. Just blue. Everywhere.

Although scared and confused, delight fills her widening eyes as she looks down in awe. Pearlescent turquoise and bottle green seas meeting isles of golden sands, framing shades of forest greens and earthy hues sweeping into land.

A perfect picture, from above.

Unlike her memories of the shadowy world left behind that sit beneath white fluffy clouds, pressing down on Earth.

She looks at home below, between gaps of clouds: gradients and contours sweep up and over vibrant green hills then drop into darkened dips like crushed velour, rich greens, and browns. Either side, yellowy-gold-green carpets gloat in pools of sunlight.

Her new sights curve around the blue planet, zooms focus, down and in, to its solid core, immovable rock edged by its opposite fluid swell of emotive water. That, seemingly separated by a fine line, water from sand and shore from land yet somehow entwined by unseen luminous wefts, merging as one.

Pearl contemplates on the elements as beings, how dependent they are, water:

She who hydrates, wildly creative, moving and rising from deep currents to reflective surfaces, filling and saturating all of life.

The rugged rock:

Anchoring, nurturing, nourishing and supporting. Earth and water, fluid and solid, perfect opposites, how their embrace and interplay perfectly understands each other's place, knowing their purpose and boundary without asking anything from one another, nor trying to change each other.

She catches herself ruminating:

Where are these thoughts coming from?

She continues:

How perfect the intelligence of nature's movement and patterns complies, confidently demonstrating its qualities in a loving, everlasting interrelationship of acceptance and balance. Enhancing, complementing each other, respective of their inherent roles.

Pearl, in reverence, senses something emerging.

"Look!" she gasps in excitement. "How She urges forth to shore, like a raging lover, busily flirting to and fro in a temptress sway."

Pearl is enthralled by this powerful, great oceanic body of liquid; indestructible while in thunderous play.

The very substance of water never destroying itself while thrashing. Crashing. Booming. And, all the while, Earth, scarred by Her erosion withstands such battering, never fights back, never ever gives up but stands completely still.

As Pearl's view of Earth widens, she is evermore mystified by her heights. Elevated by majestic beauty touching her in ways beyond her knowing when a great shadow of cloud hangs over her, threatening, stirring unease. She remembers:

Scarlett, Mr Fox? I've got to go...

Perhaps by studying a patch below it will bring her back to Earth, but all of a sudden, she hits an invisible wall of air and plummets at high-speed. Only on passing archives of cloud as it dawns on her:

I'm falling through the sky again! Like a raging torrent towards the water.

"What do you see?" The enchanting voices reappear.

"Aura!" *Where did that come from?* she asks herself, *Are you my Aura?* "I'm so glad you're back, where've you been?"

Never not there, they never left. Their whisperings are all about her, "Why do you doubt such mystery Pearl?" but she does not hear. Instead, she babbles. "Where've you been all this time? So much has happened since you left. You wouldn't believe what I've seen." She rants on and on, making noise about her lifts and drops. The elements, the colours, her terror, the beauty until realising her reverberations amplify through an empty sky – that she is without a reply.

"Are you there?"

It is only in that vast silence that she senses, and

smiles. "Ah. Okay. I'm ranting." She stops.

And she contemplates.

Am I to entice these Celestial sounds…

She checks her call, "Aura?" pushing her hearing as far as she can, attentively, awaiting a response.

But, nothing.

7

INITIATION 1

Black Light Calls

AFTER WAITING SOME time, Pearl loses hope of their return. She notices a solitary cloud ahead. It hangs amidst the vast shimmering blue all around, and yet all she sees is that speck of cloud. It carries a coldness reminding her of the same estranged feeling that first night she met Rocks where she, like the cloud, is alone, vulnerable, and exposed.

"Don't let me see you again," he warned, only to return minutes later. He liked the way she spoke and dressed. He could tell she wasn't short of money.

"You need a ride," he told her as he pulled up in his car.

"Um…" I might as well, she thought, it's no riskier than the walk home. Plus, cabbies don't pick up in this area during the day, never mind at night.

"It's not a question. It 'ent safe round 'ere, time a night an' all that," he said. "Come on. Get in. Lemme at least drop you into the civilised world."

Pearl looked up and wiped droplets from her forehead.

"Looks like rain," he smiled as he leaned over the passenger seat to open the door.

Do not get in the car, she thought when a bit of grit flew in her eye.

"Ouch." A ladybird. She rubbed her eye and mumbled, "I can't see properly."

"Somefin' buggin' ya?" He smiled, distracting her.

"Very funny." She said while entering the car.

All the signs were there. The body contractions, the collision with the ladybird, the inner voice, but she did not see nor listen to that old, wise voice even though spoken blatantly through Rocks. You could say she got in the car blindly, and off they drove into that thick, black night.

"You're shiverin'," he lulled her and turned on the heat.

She warmed up, started to relax. There's something about the motion of wheels from one place to the next, she thought, that transitory phase. To Pearl, it gave a deep, blanketing rest, of no-one to be, nowhere to go until Rocks took a wrong turn.

"Left!" she told him. He turned right.

"What did you do that for? I said left, not right."

"Relax, we're goin' on a mystery tour." He smiled. "Yea, I remember ya." He said. Remembered he had tripped her up that night in the club.

"You never said why you disappeared?"

"Well, back on ya feet dancin' wiv the girls, din't want to spoil ya fun."

"You should have. I never got to thank you properly."

He, her saviour.

♦

THE DRIVE WAS long. Pearl fell asleep. Some hours later, Rocks turned on the radio.

"North-westerly winds up to 80 miles an hour…"

"'Ere we are." Rocks smiled as he pulled up, waking Pearl.

"We're on the bloody coast?!" She couldn't wait to get out of the car. "Argh!"

"Watch it, it'll take you."

"That is one impressive gale force." She shouted, heaving the door shut.

"Don't bother closin' it, we're getting out." He told her.

They faced off the outside as it slated their defence-less humanness. After the relentless car drive she relished in meeting the raw elements, it pleased and refreshed her pores sipping the wet, Atlantic sea air, even the smell of dead fish delighted her. But dread soon washed over with realisation,

Where are we? She thought.

Seasickness waved through just by a mere glance of

the red and blue white-topped fishing boats rocking anxiously in the harbor. The sails back chatted with every wind snap that channeled through. Masts echoed like chimes with the whistling wind. And a slightly offset foghorn. Its circular misty-light flirted with the *been here before* feeling, bellowing a ceaseless mantra. It all made for an eerie quartet orchestra that creaked through the fishing village, wooing the night. The only working street lamp shone onto a green signpost and presented Newlyn, like the opening of stage curtains.

"Cornwall?"

A WILD SIGHT for those city girl eyes. A wild sight that saw the rot behind his smiling eyes.

Ah! she realised, where else better than here to pick up opiates.

Where else but a bleak and desolate place, not a sea bird in sight, beneath a hostile night, and is why every part of her sighed relief – that he eyeballed a pub across the street. Others, she thought. That made her feel safer in the dark remains of a Cornish town, battered in a storm on the edge of land.

Rocks winked, "Come," he said, crossing the road towards The Dealers Arms.

The aftermath from the gusts of bangs and flaps whipped up. "Quick. Run for your life." he joked, and she squealed when a plastic carrier drifted past like tumbleweed.

Pearl glanced around. The aliveness bashed all about abandoned second-homes yet exhausted its exhale to its very end, where every smashing blow followed a deadened silence.

They walked through a groaning, decrepit, hanging by its thread, soggy wooden gate. Then up an ally to the pub back door. Rocks tapped, tap-a-tap tap, with his knuckles. In no time, the door flew open, and they were inside. A cozy lock-in.

With the curtains drawn, who'd have known of the aliveness inside; smoked coals and drunks filled the atmosphere with spirit and warmth. A fisherman's haunt. She forgave the run-down interior for the thick, old stone walls that offered a haven. Leaped onto the first barstool she saw. Rocks beside ordered their drinks when an older man appeared on her other side.

"She'll be jumping in me grave next." He spewed.

Pearl laughed.

"She thinks I'm joking?" He said to the bar lady, dismissing Pearl, then looked straight through her, at Rocks.

"Steal my fuckin' seat why don't ya." Eyeballed Rocks for an answer.

As though silence entered, the cheery pub noise suddenly shuffled to a halt.

He looks different from the others, in his sixties maybe, but he's not lost his looks, Pearl thought, I do hope he's not who Rocks' is meeting. It was clear to her this man was not a fisherman.

Pearl then looked at the bar lady but all she received was a gaping smile, showing off her gums. Front teeth missing, both sets.

How un-lady-like Pearl thought and ushered a U-turn glance, right to left, through the pub. Horrified, that every pair of eyes met hers with gummy smiles. All their front teeth missing, both sets!

Surely not, she thought.

She looked back at Rocks, "Get me out of here, quick."

He laughed. "Don't worry. His barks' worse than his bite. You're with me now."

Ah, so he *is* the one he's meeting, she thought.

"Dan!" Rocks said to the man who spewed. "Don't be rude. This is Pearl. She's my new friend. Make her welcome."

That told him.

Then Rocks whispered in her ear, "Stay by 'is side, he'll look afta ya. E's a good'n. Promise – (winked) – "I'm gonna disappear, won't be more than ten."

"Oh, I…" She gestured herself off the barstool. In doing so, her gaze fell upon a pink rose. Just one rose inside an old vintage glass on an empty table. Its freshness upon its elegant stem inquired the air. Pearl got lost in that rose. Its sweet scent imbued all about her.

"No. Pearl. You do not want to go with him." She heard, and at the same time, "No. Pearl. You don't wanna go…" Rocks' voice overlapped the voice of the rose.

She remembered how Rocks took care of her that night she tripped in the club and how he helped her. So she warmed to his promise, nodded her head, "Okay," and warmed to Dan, by his word.

MOMENTS AFTER ROCKS left, she and Dan ordered a drink and listened to 'Al Green' *Let's Stay Together* over and over. Pearl saw Dan turn pensive as the same song replayed.

"Someone special?"

His face saddened. "You could say that."

"She still around?"

"She is, and my wife Viv knows it." He saw her awkward expression. "Oh, it's not how you think it is. Nance was my first and only real love."

Pearl didn't know what to say.

"Cut a long story short," (sighed), "I was a war baby born in New York. I met Nance. We fell in love. Sweet sixteen." He smiled. "Then, I got deported. We never made it back to each other, life was different back then. We had to move on, live apart. Eventually, I met Viv, my wife, we had a couple of kids, grown-up now," (smiled), "anyway, some years after I got a call from Nance, still in New York. You see, I told her not to contact me again, but she had to. She had to inform me about her son – our son. Twenty years of not knowing had already gone."

"All that time you never knew?"

"Nope."

"Did you ever meet or speak?"

"Oh, I wanted so much too. The one time we spoke was heartbreaking for the three of us. It upset Viv too. Our kids, mine and Viv's, began to settle with their own families. The risk of involving and upsetting all, including the grandparents," he sighed, "was too overwhelming to bear. It would have affected too many others. The whole thing had already made my wife sick."

"I'm so sorry. That must have been so difficult, but you're happy with Viv, your wife?"

"She reminds me regularly how she *knows* she's not the one. She knows she's second best."

"Is it true?"

"Yeah. It is true. I love Viv, but the truth is the truth. It's not the same love I feel for Nance. Not a day goes by I don't think about my true love in New York." His eyes filled with tears. "For fuck sake," Pearl jumped as he shouted, thumping his fist on the bar, "someone change the fuckin record." Then turned and smiled to Pearl, "Another drink?"

A few hours passed when Rocks finally returned, and Pearl was as merry and red-cheeked as the rest. He peered his head around the door, "Ready?"

◆

After The Dealers Arms

ROCKS HAD NOT spoken a word to Pearl on returning to the car.

"Can I just say, opps," stumbled into the car, "that was a long ten minutes. Where now?" she slurred as they drove away from the The Arms.

He said nothing but smiled a smug smile as they entered a heavy darkness that poured in before them. His mood changed, he seemed, unfriendly. Powerless by his sharp steer of the wheel, she panicked – where are we going, she thought. It was difficult to see through the repetitive swish-swoosh of wipers, the blurry rained-on windscreen, and as the road narrowed to the width of the car, everything closed in, even the strong aroma of fresh pine from outside. That and the fact that her ears were popping, meant that she could guess at their spiralling descent into the darkest depths of a winding forest.

Rocks freewheeled until the hostile jerk of his foot interrupted the downward flow every few seconds. On and off the brake like some sort of joke: it amused him. But as the road flattened out and the squelch of wheels trudged through splattering water Pearl sensed they'd crossed a ford. He stopped. The engine cut.

It was a dead end.

He leant over her and opened the door. "You can go if you want," he smiled.

"Sorry?"

He had given her a choice. In the middle of a dark

forested night, where would she go to? She collapsed inwardly – free-falling – crying for her deceased mother's arms, only to find herself cushioned inside that solitary cloud when her consorts and companions return.

They whisper, "Pearl. Where are you?"

Aura, is that you? I'm here, inside this cloud. It's comfortable, it's peaceful here.

"Resist this false sense of comfort, Pearl. Move your body."

The Auroras have witnessed and witness all. They are eternal. They know of her journey before and know of her journey beyond. Ever-watchful they have never not been present, but unseen by the human mind who only when broken, calls for their help.

"Put your head towards the sea below," Aura whispers.

Paralysed while airborne, Pearl stalls inside the cloud – she is not responding.

Am I upside down, sky, sea or ground-facing?

She tries moving but is disorientated. Her head tips through a backward loop and she drops, losing altitude rapidly.

"Wake up. Pearl. Keep moving. Quick, move your head down – imagine an invisible tube and push your whole body through, upside down, inside the tube, head towards the sea below you." But her guidance is not concrete. It is a sense in which she just suddenly knows what to do.

The Auroras then gently slant Pearl's position. The flat, metallic, aqua sea appears above her head, and a bottomless sky spreads below her feet. Moving out of the cloud into twilight makes the transition even eerier. Charging upside-down, headfirst, at such great speed, the air encases her in an invisible, crucible warmth, forcing her body to tilt into a sudden vertical lift.

Whoah…

Pearl then reverts to her earthly polar perspective to the usual northern hemisphere sight and effortlessly slows through a gentle glide.

"Did that just happen?" she speaks out loud.

"Do you realise the intensity of opposing forces forged you to plane out, happened because of your will?"

Overwhelmed, she does not hear.

◆

A LITTLE LATER, basking in the silence of her consort's soothing embrace, Pearl hears the whispers, "We did smile when you named us Aura, it holds the meaning *will*."

"Oh, what will?"

"Yours, of course."

She understands. She knows that she must continue to regain her will.

"And I'm Alula, we are two," they sing in unison.

Their friendship is bonding. "You were telling us

what happened with Rocks?"

"I was?" taking her mind back to that dark forested night, "Oh yes. He told me to go. Instinct told me – I have to run, but he raised his hand and I froze."

"Don't worry, I'll look after ya." He smiled his wicked way. "You like music?" he asked. "You're gonna love this," he said, and pressed play.

"It was a penetrative sound," Pearl recalls, "pounding heavy, repetitive beats inside the car, pumping rhythmically."

What is that, touching me?

Suffocated by his lurking penetrative shadow, strangely, she felt a warm breeze on her skin, and in that, soothing frequencies overlapped and harmonised those beats. As though creating a space between her body and its heaviness.

"I remember Rocks boomed a huge great laugh, uncontrollably. He laughed and laughed until his strained face wetted with tears, and he laughed so hard I couldn't tell if his laugh had turned to anguish. You've a monster in your mind, he said to me and laughed some more. His shadow lifted and in that dim light all I saw was his deceiving, rotten smile."

This confused her very much because the car then filled with light and she was not sure if she imagined his shadow penetrating her or not, but from that moment on she did everything he told her. Everything. She owed him that much, because he hadn't hurt her, she thought, so she hid beneath his shadow while he played with her mind.

"All I heard was the sun, strangely – it soothed me with a sound as it shone brightly." – (pauses) – "Do you know, Aura, it was in that radiance the sun emitted angelic choir sounds, and shimmered, just like yours."

The Auroras smile that she is becoming receptive to their gentleness beneath her distress.

Although, I cannot be sure that hidden beneath there is a light.

"That light, ever-present, neither saves nor completely protects Pearl." Aura informs, "It is only in the act of reaching out that a possible pouring of grace permeates and support. Mostly, you are not receptive to that."

"Don't you see, Pearl," Alula concludes, "it is because of your call we were able to bring comfort, but only by your call."

8

COMMUNE

Your touch, an ocean
of wakeful presence.

"THERE IS A place we can inform you of Pearl... with your consent?" Her consoles ask. "A place where you will come to *know*." Their spoken words transmit in high-pitched frequencies, a refined female softness.

"You mean home? Are you taking me home?"

No reply.

She loses balance.

Oh no! Not again...

Aura and Alula watch her tumble, then fall.

In her distress, she plummets fast. And like the Mothers arms swoops her child up from the ground, Pearl is enveloped and cradled. Her body pulses by their ethereal, binaural sounds. And faintly, in the farthest distance, a soothing whisper.

"Shift your gaze to the horizon, let yourself ascend with our thermals. It is a great effort at first, Pearl. Use your will."

They watch as she shifts her gaze towards the horizon. Rising as a bird, she glides on the thermals. With their support, it is effortless. Over the ocean, she admires the white ruffles that lace the edge off the shore. Fascinated yet brilliant quandary draws her out to deeper waters. Silvery ripples beneath the sun trail like twinkling fireflies, and Pearl thinks of Scarlett's silver dress.

"It's me." She hears.

Scarlett?

"Where are you?" Pearl calls out.

Memories of Scarlett distract her from her guides.

"It's happening again, Quick. I'm falling!"

Every time she listens to the constructs of the thinking mind, she falls. Of course, never to the ground. Her consorts enable her to feel the intensity of the fall to go beneath its surface. Beneath the illusion to awaken, and enliven, to access and enact her will by herself. Only then does she sense her consoles swathe and lift.

"Be wild and carefree like the ocean, Pearl, but try not to recede with the tidal wave of thought – this will keep you in a constant swing of ups and downs. Even the rise and fall of the waves break free through Her emotive swell into immensely thunderous, explosive outbursts." Aura whispers.

"Her?"

Pearl's quest travels the air to the ocean. She feels reverberations hush all about her as the oceans respond.

"Wait, did you hear that, Aura?" Goosebumps shiver

all over her. "Did you hear the whispers of the ocean?"

"What did She say?" Alula asks.

"I am powerless," She says about herself. She says she is dependent on the moon's circuitry loops. And now, she is saying, "I am a magnetic expression of *Her* silent song."

The sound of the ocean increases, Ssh, "I, am the tumult of Her silence."

Although I cannot be sure I understand...

"She, the sea, and the moon. Listen to all that you cannot see. Go beneath the currents for your *knowing* to rise from the stillness of Her depth." Aura whispers.

Pearl listens.

Alula continues, "Her silent song is an invitation to enter that space, to receive Her."

"Receive what, must I receive something to return home? And who is She, do you mean Scarlett?"

Aura and Alula pause before continuing:

"There are hidden treasures of nature, inherent in you, appearing magical, should you become illuminated by Her grace, they'll ripen as Her expression, through you. That can come about through deep attentive, introspection. You see, the power is in the silence and is what renders Her absorption. This is the rising of Her silent song."

"Oh, *you're* the silent song of the moon... not my Aura?"

No reply.

The Auroras penetrate the illusions of Pearl's mind and senses but shooting pains in her body veil the informed voices.

Ugh, my body hurts all over, it's heavy, like leaden.

"Pearl, stay with us." Waves of love pulse and vibrate through her entirety.

"I just, don't understand."

"Then try not too. Surrender to the air. Listen for the revelatory deeper knowing that arises from in-between the two worlds."

"In-between?"

"There is something ever-present, alive in the air. Listen. You will perceive much more when you still yourself in-between the worlds, for that which penetrates through you is in the air. And the air is in you. Merge with the elements Pearl."

"Hmm," she nods. "So, I can slip in-between two worlds by merging with you?"

This dream is cool.

But this is no dream. The deep-down inside of knowing this is why questions probe:

"What is there to see, who *are* you, why do you keep disappearing from me?"

"Hello?"

Pearl's echo is her only response. She ponders her view from the shore to inland, seeking false comfort through the familiarity of her earthly home. She fantasises about the chaos of life stories etched on the

Earth's surface. She looks below, paving eyes along the criss cross rows of endless streets that shrink and narrow as she soars, awestruck, until a sudden noise bombards her:

What is that?

She hears what she hears when back on Earth. Insignificant debates and chats. Hovering on the ground and filling up space and then rising like a mist, an edifice of thoughts, voices overlap and tower. The loudening of arguments, disagreements, and laughter weave in and out of sociability, activity, and circumstance. Over that, the constructs of technology, workforce, and industry. And over that, road traffic, all emitting and layering as one multi-directional sound weft.

It's a raging conflict down there. No wonder. No one listens to one another.

"There is a softness in Her dense matter, feel our warmth fill you."

Sorry, what did you say? (Distracted by wailing cries). *I hear someone… people in pain, hold on, Earth is crying…*

There is unbearable pain in her ears,

Ugh, it's hard, grinding, heavy material, raising her hands she covers them.

It sounds so destructive, why would we do that, why do live like that? wincing, she scrunches her face in a ball.

"What's going on? Hello? Aura, Alula, where are you?" (Demands).

Why are you not beside me?

"Hello?" (Hollers).

But they are beside her – so close, only she does not hear their soothing sounds over the suffering world penetrating her. She does not feel their warming softness and subtle caress. Unable to perceive, full of doubt. All she sees and hears is the noise pollution that weighs, pulling her down. Exhausted, she falls.

Show me what to do?

As she quietens to listen, it brings about a surrender to that fall. Then the warming breeze swathes and lifts her again.

Thank you, thank you. It really is a relief to know you. She relishes, and bathes in their consolation but still, she does not realise that her consorts are responding to her thoughts.

♦

Later,

WHAT WAS ALL that I heard?

"Your cries, sufferings, and everyone else's. Its collective, Pearl. Earth *is* crying."

"The awakening of your suffering will enable you to see more. Grieving will open more space for you to listen more deeply. The Earth cries to be heard. Each individual must seek their own will to heal."

And she is listening.

"There is a depth of beauty in pain, the destructions

and its repercussions have to be acknowledged to *will* something new. Do you see?"

And she sees.

I do, it hurts so much though.

"Then soften, close your eyes."

And she does. She feels her palms lifting and they are placed over her ears, her eyes, and she receives a pooling of warmth.

◆

AS PEARL CONFIDES her suffering, she feels lighter, haven given herself space, a deep silent air push up through her, clearing out rights and wrongs, should's and don'ts. Comforted, she starts to let go. She no longer sees the city's circus acts via circuitry entanglement, where wefts of human traffic networks through tunnelled roofs for rats. No longer hears the never-ending buzz of swishing traffic, blaring hoots, yelling, and shouting. She starts to let go of what pains her. The complex and futile stories of sadness, fear, loss, the growing gain of desire turn greed, or whatever struggle and trauma life had drawn on the face of victims. Although still on the surface, she is without the usual mundanity of never resolving ground politics and analytical preoccupation, the control, manipulation, exploitation, the dictation. All trivia, and all that matters, dissipates. As she relishes more and more, pushing further out, into the wide shimmering blue, in that silence, her breathing expandable body 'pops'.

Silence.

"You hear it, yes." The Auroras whisper.

My skin, it feels like of a tunic peeling up and off my body, what's happening?

She awakens by the naked flame of the air, a kindling power to which she surrenders and slips out of her skin-like dress.

We're merging?

The Auroras watch as the veils subtly and gradually peel, gently revealing her nakedness.

My entire face! Oh! My eyes, and scalp are lifting off, I'm light and headless again.

And in a flash, countless useless memories and thoughts dissolve by the electric charge of the ocean below, lighting her up. Her eyes, translucent.

The visibility up here is so utterly pristine.

Her vision pans out to 360-degrees. As she forgoes the physical outline of her body, in that very moment, the sky and ocean merge as one, and a wide-open blue unfurls from inside Pearl.

Yes. We Have merged! I just know it. This. Is. Incredible. There is so much deep peace, so much spaciousness.

Her pores drink in the virgin air, as a silent sky imbues from inside and she glides through untouched space where no earthly body ever touched before.

Aura and Alula continue to watch, weaving within

and around, allowing the gift of freedom to pervade her. While the pouring of liberation fills her with vast empty sky, she realises, that she herself, a quietude of air; becomes the sky!

My eyes are expanding beyond all measure of distance and direction, leaving all stories of duality, past and future to vanish.

How can this be, I'm unending, and pulsating in a bountiful, indescribable pleasure!

Suddenly, "I can touch… whoah! Aura! I am the horizon! Aura, are you there?" She wants to tell her guides.

No beginning, no end, if not for the streak of sunlight thrown on the breathless ocean, defining above and below. Pearl's focus looks down, and polarity, form and structure start to architect, swiping that quietude of air.

No! Please, don't stop.

She finds herself separated from that vast spaciousness of pure being-ness as she shrinks back into her body. Although her awestruck wonder is short-lived; her total detachment of earthly existence means that, on returning, no question about it, she is with altered eyes.

◆

AS THE BACK of her mind persists and tugs, quickly forgetting her truest comfort and caress, she starts to contract and the next wave of air sways her back and forth in turbulence again. She falls.

How many times must I rise and fall, this is exhausting, and why does space do that, lift and throw me around?

"Fall into *us* Pearl. Use your will out of these lifts and drops for something new to form. Remember the invisible tube?"

In the thick of intensity, quick to forget such a thing is possible, she loses patience.

"I just want to go back now, I want to go home."

As if in response, the sea gathers her liquid material and slams her white-laced ruffles against the shore. She is the fire of a flamenco dancer who grabs her lavish dress, consuming Pearl.

Oh God, "Is She angry with me?"

Yes. She is angry.

What I have done, did I say something wrong?

"This, a concerning anger that wants to nurture. She wants you to want to fully wake from your suffering, so you can engage." Aura whispers.

Oh, She wants me to bear with the elements, like some sort of commune?

"Is that what you mean by merging with the elements, to talk with the ocean? I thought you said I only have to call?" Pearl asks aloud.

She waits for answer.

"Hello… I'm calling you!" Stretching her vision inland.

She ponders in a world of her own, so much so, she

forgets she's waiting for an answer.

Just then,

Hold on, you can hear me! The naked flame of the air, she thinks, *You've been replying to me all along – to my thoughts. I should have realised.*

She tests a quick inner soundcheck:

I don't need to speak to you aloud, do I?

No reply.

You are that subtle? Realising now, she is never not heard. *I know you are here, help me to see what I need, show me how you want me to move?*

And – *whoosh* – the fluttering sounds reappear, sweeps and lifts her up, whispering their weaves of silvery veils inside and out of her being.

"Ah! You're back!"

Aura never left.

"Space is not *doing* anything. It's not a conspiracy or myth, Pearl, but responds and is always available, even when on the ground. Whispers of the elements rise from the earth and travel through the air and the waters fluidity. The flame hungers for the naked air to be ignited, to purify and show true light, in which the dance of life shapes and reforms. Listen deeply to what you cannot see."

Pearl receives.

"And will us." Aura continues, "It is what drives the call – your only device as an expression of will." Alula joins in. "It's important to understand the way you *will* us you can think and talk yourself in and out of anything. Here."

She nods pensively.

"Remember do not doubt the unseen, Pearl, even in your calls." Aura and Alula smile.

Through attentive listening, she merges deeper by the swish and swirl of invisible forces of fury, joy, and caress. Moving as fluid as the ocean herself but in the air. She continues to expand with her eyes lit, stretching her vision vastly.

I'm getting wider.

The more she listens, she expands. The more she sees, she receives. But she must will her consorts, something only she alone can render.

And so she heads into an entire oceanic-sky landscape, which divides into two: dark and light. On her left, a black-blue sea holds the weight of cloud above. Beside its darkness, golden beams light up a bright, pastel-blue sky on her right. And beneath her, a flock of seagulls fly by, turning their belly-to-back transitions in perfect sync. Swathed by the strike of the sun's reflection, all dressed up in golden flashes – the smiling sun, flickers across their breasts. And their smiling eyes too, glide smoothly, in and out of air currents, turning their white feathers gold. Pearl's smiles of hope tickle the gulls as she reaches out with her hand.

"Hey, come back!" She is made breathless by her call out loud, which is swallowed by the sky.

Pearl tries with all her might to move towards the gulls who effortlessly fly away.

"See how much fun you're having when you relax."

Until now, life had been tedious.

Mmm… I am ready.

High in the sky, with ocean in front, Pearl glances over her shoulder back to land; to the chaos on Earth behind her. The place she once knew as home rapidly shrinks into stillness, but for the sun that flashes through cloud-breaks, striking mirrored lakes to wink. The Earth twinkles as she soars into the distance. Soaring between stark contrasts of shadow and light, its breathtaking sight is enough to make her let go of her nostalgic grasp on home.

"Do you know your deepest fears, Pearl?" The Auroras ask.

I suppose… I thought I was going to die.

"You think you're alive?"

This is a dream, isn't it…? I've been here before in my dreams.

"Pearl, don't you remember why you're here?

9

HIDDEN BENEATH

Just as a kiss cannot be had by one's own lips,
the Self cannot be touched.

PEARL WARMS MORE to Aura and Alula. After all, if she is stuck in a dream, she will need their help out – if to return home. She faces the horizon of her future sky. Since she is more established in silent communication with the ethers, she no longer speaks aloud but transmits fully through thoughts. They have been waiting.

Pearl asks about the silent song of the moon,

"She is both fruit-bearer and shadow-keeper to those whose calls are heard. Perhaps you have noticed Her guidance?" the Auroras go on, "even in the black of sky you may meet the secret light."

Pearl ruminates.

"The enveloping darkness is a grace that offers the promise of renewal. But you have to go there. You have to enter the dark to see what you cannot."

You are being so elusive right now.

"The dark mystery will lead you to your innermost

secret of unknown truths. Pearl, whatever you find is for you."

And so she evokes the mysterious unknown by pushing her deep listening into that thick, rich silence in search of the furthest sound beyond. Not quite sure what I'm looking for, she thinks, when doubt arises, and suddenly right before her, a harrowing cloud appears, shrouding the turquoise sea in great blackness.

So I'm to go ahead, towards that black cloud?

"Remember, in the dark, the secret light is seen. Know this, Pearl. There is no need for you to contract when these opposites intensify, know you are simply moving paradigm. Be fierce and steady as a flame, for that which you embrace will transcend."

But it's a mighty, intrusive presence. The great sky closing in sandwiches her between dense layers of cloud. Instinct makes her peer over her shoulder, through a hole in the cloud, where she catches a fading glimpse of the sun's backlight. It reaches inland and there is a patchwork of golden sands, glowing beneath a blazing blue.

"You see, light is behind you..." the whispers encourage as she continues flightpath into the cold dark. With the wind radically increasing, Pearl is tossed and taken, gust by gust, like a spinning propeller.

"It will feel like you're losing control with nothing to grasp on to, in this anti-gravity field." The ethers whisper through the wind.

Show me now how I should move?

And as she enters silence to retrieve subtle response, she is informed. She just knows how to shape and morph her body with the air dynamics while focusing on the horizon.

♦

SHE GLIDES ON towards her distant future, towards a milky cloud-bank mountain. Stirring from its stillness a tremendous curling wave rolls forth.

Oh no, it's changing, and charging towards me. Again!

She cannot fathom its growing width and height as it closes in, it's at least a hundred miles wide.

You don't get much of a break up here, do you?

Raising its alpine glow up from the horizon, the cloud face hurls towards her at immeasurable speed. She enters a wall of wind and her hair pulls from her scalp, becoming excitably taut. There is a cool freshness seeping inside, awakening billions of follicles. Her eyes are watering and streams of tears wet her face, and the air pressure is immensely vigorous. As the oncoming cloud traffic approaches, she uses all her effort to swerve when…

Argh, I'm moving backwards…No…!

She thrusts her arms out in an attempt to guard against it.

It's devouring me.

Thrown and torn by its supreme presence.

Argh…!

With sky-wide eyes, she gasps, overspilling with fright. She clears her arms through the air, sweeps them alongside her body, and extends her toes. Her body long and thin – sharp like an arrow – steers a fast forward speed.

The sea, it's raging in the opposite direction.

"That's not the sea moving, you are in flight."

Then suddenly, she halts, opens her mouth and stares in disbelief at utter peace spreading across the cloudless sky. She glances at her body.

I can't believe it. I'm through the other side.

And all in one piece, head to toe. Stunned, she turns 180 degrees to the airspace behind only to see an iridescent wispy cloud edge that had passed straight through her, rushing towards the land.

That had to have been tens of hundred miles wide, yet took seconds to pass. And I'm still here. "You passed the edge of a storm. You only experienced its thin, superficial layer by the time it reached you. You'll go through much denser, more vigorous ones soon."

Thanks for the warning!

Intense pain shoots up her spine. *Arghhh!*

"Don't worry, Pearl, you'll get used to the velocity." They smile.

"Velocity? Who *is* this? What are you, what am I talking to?"

"Let go of your earthly body Pearl. Do not let the

elements perturb you, for there are unseen powers. There is much here you can retrieve. When the wind takes you, embrace, as steady as the background of blue sky who hosts the invisible force of winds."

Just then, a corridor of cloud opens right before her.

"Go, move your way in."

As she shapes her way through the uncharted cloud-ark, its grandeur folds and closes her in from behind. It's as if the sky touches and imbues her every micro inward-being. She disappears. No sooner is she enveloped inside, she simultaneously unfolds outwardly, as a cloudscape herself. Freely exploring the aerodynamics of her body inside dense cloud, she sees her moving shadow sit on circular rainbows.

Is that my shadow chasing me or am I chasing my shadow?

She becomes so lost in sky play that a sudden *whoosh* compasses her flightpath 180 degrees back-seaward, leaving land behind.

Unawares of the whispers piloting her direction she continues her flight through a sweet tube of wind. It blows from behind her ears. Riding waves of air without a care in the world she surfs towards the ever increasing gigantic jewel in the sky. Even though it is sinking below a purple band of horizon, Pearl, raised above, sees its ceaseless rays fanning 360 degrees.

Is THIS the secret light?

Its opulence throw shards of fluorescent lights, a

widening treasure before her eyes. There are glowing amber-pinks, rippled orange pleats and neon reds streamlining and shattering open the whole sky. And there are trains of lavender clouds with golden lining. They pass by proudly, as if to approve and welcome her.

The light is incredible up here.

"Your eyes are mirroring the ever-transmuting sky."

It's utterly breathtaking.

The Auroras weave their smiles all about her.

She glides high above the sundown. There are dark clouds contrasting with bright and liberating heavens while beneath, the yawning waves soothe a twilight sea. And behind her, a pillow of fog smudges the edge of land. Its purple dusk releases a night chill as the ground dims into darkness.

I'm in-between seasonal skies. She tells the Auroras. *An ever-rising, honey glow ahead lures me into its orange brilliance. Its afterglow far-reaching land behind gradually draws the night, and the phenomena up here, ever-changing, even now, a snowy white wonderland. And down there, on the ground… I know it's oppressive. How can I go back when this warming delight ahead lures me?*

Pearl distances from the cold hardness of ground, far and out of reach; she is a tiny silhouette in a huge sunset sky. Having come this far, not knowing whether she will ever return, immersed in raw elements, her journey in-between begins. As she lifts higher the horizon wanes. And she accelerates vertically, the Earth's sphere falls away from her as she moves closer, beyond – towards what's hidden. High in the fresh black of space the anchored sundown sits omnipresent, basking in its light.

10

MOON MIRROR

In awe of the ineffable, wonder in delight.
Subtle push lifting feet, swaying through the night.
Softly, Beloved, I become such a way
Guided by your numinous sight.
The unveiling luminosity, circling in my eyes.
Moon glowing on my face, wander through the night.
Light up All there is to see,
Ocean to mountain lake, be still enough for me.

I'M FLOATING ABOVE Earth's stratosphere.

"You see."

Hmm?

"How you don't have to use your eyes to *really* see. You're seeing through feeling, the same way you feel our smiles."

If only I could see your face, please show me…

While traversing the dark abyss a sudden throw of light flashes before her. The formless voice transmutes itself into a moon, a visible consort, giving Pearl spotlight reference.

I see you! You're moving with me!

"You are never alone, Pearl."

She feels the warming swathe of sheer silk like substance wrap around her shoulders. They are weaving their dulcet tones within and all around her. Pearl's bedazzled eyes smile wide in delight alongside her perfectly round, silver-gold consorts, whose stark stream of light navigates her flightpath West to East.

With her consorts, she travels through the air, over sleepy night seas where the arc of the Milky Ways sits on the black water abyss, its reflection forms a circle. She journeys night long through cosmic rings of stardust in endless black space until sunrise lights up a grand opening of moving skies. She sees her reflection in the mirrored glass shores below.

That's strange, I was in space, now I'm flying through Earth!

Over arid deserts that rasp her parched, aching throat. She looks down at trains of clouds – and at their shadows beneath. Slivering like antique-gold snakes, cooling the burning sands. The desert floor winks like water's surface beneath the sun. She swoops to quench her thirst, only to find no end of dehydrated rivers that flow and wink once she is airborne again.

Ah, a mirage.

"To rehydrate, you need only absorb the moisture from the air." The Auroras smile, and there is another switch: Rich, velvety black.

I'm back in space!

Then over forests, where clusters of trees point upwards like giant pine cones, prodding the air. Then again, sees herself from space, through the stratosphere, she travels with the moons.

Is this possible... I'm in two places at once?

Over mounds of sunset cities, ancient raised towns dot the land pink like grouped flamingos. And over valleys, where ferocious winds are fierce yet bulky mountain-muscles stand stoic.

She never knows, or takes for granted, the changing conditions, she has learned to respect the elements. For there are times the elements are kind and other times severe; unforgivingly harsh. From blustery showers, hard-hitting hails and downpours. And rumbles that shake and crack the sky, to soothing, nourishing and comforting, warming airwaves.

But no one time do the elements ever appear the same, each one a character of its own. There are times she is without heading; sandwiched between dense cloud layers, and then other times her lucid eyes travel a thousand miles ahead of future skies. There are times when she loses herself inside sparkling clouds where the rains fall horizontally – in wonderment of the crystal pathways traversing a glistening sky. Hours, days go by on Earth time as she passes through cloud corridors where no one direction is ever again.

She is familiar with but never knows all the sensations of cloud formations, for new ones are constantly emerging. Those with heavy moods and evaporating tears, some oozing utter peace while others chatter the haunt of echoes. They come and go. There are towering clumpy ones; whose thunderous, stormy ice-rocks stab and smack, ripping layers of skin. And there are wispy, transparent ones that sheen and light her face. They come to go.

There are daunting clouds who dominate and take precedence of her mind, pushing and shoving; their façade soon vaporises when the all-present shimmering-blue blazes through. They take up space and always give it back. They are visitors who do not claim the sky. They service – for instance, when they shower they do to purify, to reset and balance the planets' psyche.

But it is the cloud-colony of flying discs who hover over mountaintops like spaceship guards who terrify Pearl from the inside out.

As she approaches the solemn range from above, its solitary cortex stands sombre.

Those towering cliff faces are rather unfriendly.

"It is here a part of you must die, Pearl." Alula's whispers stroke Pearl's hair, lifting her highest peaks within. Not for the weak nor half-hearted, there is something greatly terrifying about this extraordinary range.

Here! is where you wanted to take me?

"What is it you fear?" they ask.

They're casting heavy shadows all over me.

"Try not feel estranged or perturbed, remember, appearances of passing phenomena deceives. Behind all faces always exists a great love, unconditionally, like the vast blue sky. That space always loves," hushed Alula and Aura.

She feels a tremor in her body as she pushes and pulls in a rumbling sky over mountain peaks; their range and depth resembling the inner lobes of a human brain.

Why am I not waking? I should go now – it's time to go home.

"Try not to resist, nor let fear take hold. Soon you can rest."

The Auroras give her a boost and wrap their electro-magnetic wefts, fuelling her heart. A courage fuel. And off she soars, she floats fantastically above terrific peaks, enchanted by the glory of yet more phenomena. Gliding over glistening gold, snow-capped mountaintops who project prisms of razor-light beams into the macrocosmic sky.

This is impossibly mesmerising, I can touch the moon, and the stars…

Her skin, luminous with dewy sparkles, as stars ooze through every pore. There are organised diagrams of light that streamline the night canopy, and the moon butters the night sky bright. Basking in that very light of darkness and sky frolics she forgets herself; content in constellations – paving new threads of happiness. Then she notices the moon reflecting on the mountains' lake plateau just below.

Ah, a perfect mirror of the moon!

As golden bright as can be, the circular entirety is pillared by bronzed trees. Dripping with golden leaves, their tall, thin reflections stretch across the mirrored lake and meet in the centre like the spokes of a wheel. There are sparkling clusters of pink-quartz everywhere, just everywhere; around the lake's edge, trailing every untrodden path towards the mountain valleys. And, hidden deep within the mountain's lobes, an entire labyrinth of synapses and neurons conducting sparks of electric neon-blue, pulsing – rhythms of pathways throughout the entire range. Only the Celestial eye can witness such a dazzling sight. It is said, by the Celestial sounds, to be the subconscious part of Earth's brain.

I've never seen anything like it.

Not even in her dreams.

"It's time to drop down now," Alula informs her.

Pearl eases her descent from the cosmic sky as the formless voices guide her.

"Brace yourself," she hears. "We go down!" they said. "Head down towards Moon Mirror. She will show you what's behind your eyes."

Pearl looks blankly.

"To remember…" Aura affirms.

Pearl forgoes the unexplained, and with a subtle body swerve, dives through the air's harsh surface. It's a painful transition, bouldering towards Moon Mirror from altitude, at speed, over a thousand miles an hour. Her body shudders, the air pressure vigorous, and her skin prickled by the stab of elements, but she surpasses and torrents like a rocket. Silver trails of shooting stars stream from her periphery as she charges, head down. She passes sheer cliff-faces during her furious descent, rains of emotion washing over her when, suddenly, she slows into a stall, her heart pumping rapidly.

"Can we *not* do that again?" she says aloud, dishevelled, hovering over Moon Mirror. "My breath is outside my body, see."

"Pearl, your eyes are wildly windswept and the stars fall from your hair. Try to feel this aliveness. Your sight is 360 vision now, and yes, your heart throbs and shimmers beyond your aura but dear Pearl, see," advised the warm whispers. "Look directly into the stillness of Moon Mirror, feel the aliveness in Her presence."

As she looks down she sees her reflection, and right beside her, Rocks emerges. Moon Mirror reflects her movie-mind of sequential events, in detail, taking her back in time.

Mr Fox, in my home?

She watches as Rocks laced her food with opiates, the time he prepared food for her while she got dressed. He split a cheese chunk in two, used the pinpoint of a knife to make a hole on each side, and inserted a pill into one hole closing the other on top as a lid. Then carefully pierced a cocktail stick through, fixing the two halves together. Voilà!

Oh. His infamous cheese parties. I had no idea.

Which is the reason she didn't remember any of the following.

She was sprawled on her living room floor, in and out of mind-altering states, when Rocks chucked the white plastic bag on her lap.

"'Ave a look for yourself then." His sweet mood turned threatening. Those quick to anger nasty turns, a symptom she no longer noticed. She opened the bag and looked inside. A white mound threw out a cloud of dust and tickled her nose.

"I knew it," she frothed at Rocks. "You set me up on a deal in the service station. You let me unknowingly take the stash?" Her slurred voice croaked in every effort to raise itself, stifled, as her body tried to move. "How could you?"

"You set yourself up, Pearl," Rocks sniped with a wicked laugh. "This is your inheritance, you *gave* it to *me*. In fact, you handled your inheritance all by yourself, even put it in the bag."

"You're lying."

"Keep watching, Pearl."

The voices lovingly swathe and caress her as Moon Mirror reveals more, further back in time, to the scene at the service station.

Rocks, inside a neglected telephone box, hid a distance away but close enough to keep his eye on Pearl, holding the plastic bag, waiting.

"I'm not gonna be set up again, not this time," Rocks muttered to himself, anxious he'd been tipped again by an undercover drug squad.

Those buried memories, flashback, and begin to return:

He muttered some more: "I'll stay out of sight and watch from here. I'm not gonna go down, not again. She can look after herself, she'll be alright."

He put me up for trade for exchange of my arrested heartbeats. How could he? I knew it. He cares for nothing, no-one but himself and my money.

"Keep watching, Pearl," Aura and Alula encourage her.

Rocks, who continued to watch from afar, saw her drop the bag.

"What the, what is she doing?" he cursed Pearl. "Pick up the bag."

She'd bumped into a man... then immediately after him, *oomf* another man bumped into her after picking up the bag she dropped with cash inside – *her* cash. He swapped the bags. And there was the transaction. It happened so fast, it confused her. And Rocks, who'd been watching from afar waited for the all-clear, then fleetingly with but little guilt, rushed over and snatched the bag from her.

She hears Pops voice: "The treasure of truth is above

the sky."

He's the one I spoke with at the bar in the Basement Club? Pop. Is he following me?

"He is not following you, Pearl. You often sense it as a sort of, déjà vu, you call it. Pop caused a distraction in that time was altered. Fortunate for you, you were receptive at that moment. Officials arrived, as you were leaving. Time would have had you in a different circumstance. The one you saw unfold in the wing mirror. Arrested and charged with the goods Rocks deceived and used you for as bait."

Pearl remembers Pop, "If it wasn't for me you'd be…"

Doing time.

Meanwhile, Rocks re-emerges in Moon Mirror, this time inside the Basement club.

"Who's she takin wiv… Herself?" He muttered. "She's lost it. I gotta get her out of 'ere – she's a total liability in this state. I can' 'ave this. I can' 'ave her drawin' attention to me wiv the squad on m'back. I do-not wanna get busted again." He rushed over to Pearl at the bar, grabbed her forcibly. "Come on, you're coming wiv me. I'm taking you 'ome."

So he didn't see Pop? Both times he didn't see Pop?

"Close your eyes, Pearl, concentrate, beyond your senses." The Auroras support her. "Your guides are alive and ever with you, Pearl. They intervene for your attention, to wake you. They speak through many forms in whatever possible ways to reach you. The human appearance of Pop was like something of a mirage that manifests for your physical eyes to perceive, but even then your physical limitations deny and doubt. Humans even express 'seeing is believing.' But it's the opposite. The unseen is very much alive and not through vanishing acts or words, Pearl, which is why they tug on your instinct. Yet it is so difficult for you, and is why instinctive feelings stay with you and never go *until* you see."

Pearl looks around.

Who, where?

Then gasps. She feels, sees, senses shape and form, but it disappears as fast as it appears.

Yes! It feels so real yet I cannot touch it, and then it fades just like a dream when waking up.

◆

PEARL AND THE Auroras continue communication, floating high in the ether. Tired as she is, Pearl rests her millpond eyes to float upon the healing wisdoms of Moon Mirror, watching the fast-forward motion of her events.

Just beyond the water, in front of a cave, sits a pretty fox. His orangey-red coat reflects over Moon Mirror. He looks fantastic beneath the rose-gold moon in the blue sky. Staring cunningly into her eyes:

I can't look away, he's drawing me into the cave.

He pulls her toward him like a magnet.

"Go, Pearl, he wants to show you something," Aura encourages her.

She follows him inside.

He's busy, shuffling something around, compartmentalising, organising.

"Rocks, is that you, what are you doing?" she asks out loud.

"He doesn't hear you, Pearl," Aura says.

He doesn't see me either. We're in the living room of my home, he's looking straight into the fireplace.

She sees how he had made himself at home in hers. Using her key, entered and left, entered and left, many times over. She sees behind all doors in her home, inside cupboards and beneath floors too. There are hidden stashes, tightly compressed. Wraps are individually sealed, neatly with cellophane and tape. It's the work of a seamstress. Inside each wrap are hundreds, thousands of pills stamped with happy and menacing faces. There are microdots, liquids, rocks, powders, all sealed (and dated). A narcotics sweetshop of opiates and stimulants, and there are copious amounts.

The tapping and shuffling inside my walls. It was Mr. Fox all along, stashing all that gear, cutting and washing, in my home?

"Pearl, look closer, that is not Rocks in your home."

Dan! Is that Dan? What...?

"Pearl, Dan is Rocks' father."

I feel sick.

She closes her eyes but she wants to know everything and so continues, bravely, to see through the fabricated worlds. Of his lies. The Auroras forever by her side inform her:

"These outer worlds are all but reflections of your inner world Pearl and not easy to see and is why your reflections flash as a lighthouse does. Miss the first time, second or third, these flashes will continue to circle. Until you see."

Pearl thinks back.

The Silver flashes…

And then comes Scarlett, emerging from Moon Mirror, handling Pearl's inheritance money with Rocks, and she *sees* them.

I don't understand… the money…

They kiss like lovers.

◆

PEARL STRETCHES AND contracts like plasticine in the sky. There are great cumulonimbus clouds, towering, thousands of feet within. As she resists, the cloud towers whip around. She cannot breathe. The pressure builds, her skin is humid and sticky, and she implodes.

"Pearl, breathe." Alula and Aura soothe her.

Unbridled in destruction, she does not hear, and so

there are times her consoles and consorts expand out in silent witness.

NOW IS ONE of those times.

SHE CONTINUES TO erupt outwardly, gurgling, expanding in all directions like live culture. The Aurora's watching. Clouds of delusion evaporate from Pearl, one by one, from her inside out, collapsing shadows of betrayal, clearing the atmosphere of her mind, but stormy clouds of anger, rage, turmoil and hurt lurk in her periphery. Encircling, they sit in lingering threat. This isn't over yet, and she knows it.

THE AURORAS MAKE their presence felt, gently soothing Pearl with their swathes.

"Next time a gust of anger whips inside play with the wind. This anger with Rocks, projecting arrows of thoughts like darts, is not the right way, Pearl. This is not a conquest. We understand you are hurt, but those darts have a way of navigating back, staying stuck in your heart. Who then will remove these?"

Oh, I…

"Your unspoken thoughts are ever-present. You will see nothing is separate. In this moment, your holding pattern swings to and from polar opposites where your silent broadcast is heard and felt by all. Do you remember what Pop told you about conversion of energies?"

Alula continues, "emotions can be like a tremor, a spasm, like when bursting into tears. As soon as the tremor arises, absorb it. It is fuel for the heart. As soon as anger arises, locate it in your body. Find out where is lives then draw it into your heart."

How... When did Scarlett become involved? She was handling my inheritance – my money, with Rocks? I never once saw them together until the last night in The Basement Club. I just don't understand.

"Scarlett, really?" Alula asks. "You are the destroyer of Pearl. The bad in you seeks to kill your good."

Pearl sits beside herself. Confused, she thinks back.

ALULA ADDS, "LET this hurt melt. Give yourself time; You will see every fall meets a lift, and you will know how to turn the whole thing upside-down and move beyond all polarity. You will no longer swing into one way without confiding your ally of discernment."

Deep inside I know. But these truths are still a painful blow. *How can this deep-down-inside-of-me full of so much love let such things happen? I mean, how could I just not...*

"Say anything?" The Auroras pause. "Illusions are powerful and strong, Pearl, and can kill. Even though *you know* you still you put yourself there. It is what you humans call denial."

Yes. She turns pensive. *Most would say I'm weak.*

"What do most know, Pearl? You followed a greater power navigating you to this point, though in exchange for your physical Existence." Aura tells her.

Exchange?

"Our currency of exchange here, Pearl, is truth and love. Meaning, that which it does not resonate with eventually falls away. Rocks used you, unawares, as his accomplice. Consequently you lost your sight, and faith, and this made it so easy for him."

Once again, Pearl embraces her reflections in Moon Mirror. It is the last time she will look at that face, that old face of the past, smothered and deceived by Rocks' mist that appeared to hold a somewhat mystic presence. He, the dark cloud of her underworld, hid behind the silvery, smooth complexion of fiery dragons of an opiate den. All the while she, was smitten by his trickery. Oh, how he possessed her. For she succumbed to his subliminal ways; of the summer warmth held in her hands to the strike of lightning through her veins. She was at his mercy, unable to resist the provocative, opaque curves and scents that seduced. Of a shining armour that flirted around her lips, arousing nausea and shudders before she plunged into cascading realms of velvet brown, of undulating darkness drawn to cessation. There, her pinned existence wiped flat over an opaque field of serenity and smothered her pain.

◆

IT'S A WIDE-BLUE expanse across an estuary-sky of thin

ice-cloud. Pearl skates on air, she pirouettes, careful not to fall through the blue of tidal inlets.

"Pearl." Whispers awaken her by tumbling her like a duvet shaken in mid-air. She loses her grip, and the blue slips through her fingers, and back in free-fall she plummets towards Moon Mirror.

Pearl watches her microscopic reflection enlarge, charging towards her new face.

"Steady, Pearl, we've got you." With their swooping grace, she hangs above a cloud.

"What do you feel?"

I can't describe what I feel.

"Try, Pearl."

One moment I'm in a push and pull of heavy and painful resistance. Up and down and all around, letting go and then not, and...

"Go on..."

And then I feel liberated, seeing and feeling from an elevated view. I experience all of life interconnected on multiple levels of every thought, move, and interaction as being of the same thread. And then...

"Yes. Go on, Pearl."

And then again my body constricts and pulls by fear...

It suddenly strikes her, *Is this a passing... Am I dead?*

11

UNDYING DEATH

Safe and warm, pink storm. Black calls.

"IT'S TIME TO go higher, Pearl," the Auroras tell her.

A deeper fall, you mean... she smiles reluctantly. A misty air of silent frustration and refuse trails from her nostrils – she wants to think alone.

They remind her again that it's through feeling that brings her closer to their presence.

I know. I cannot hide from you. I can't do this anymore, I just can't, I'm tired.

"You are so close," Alula encourages a warming sense around her.

What to...?

"Home, of course."

Pearl lifts through the fresh upper skies. Above mountaintops and silvery clouds, above the cold, and above the moon. She contemplates on its luminosity, the power of its brightness penetrating the dusk below.

"You see that sinkhole?" Aura asks.

With the Earth at her feet, Pearl looks down, beyond

myopic sight, all the way down, to where an eerie emptiness hangs in the air but for the bats flit-in-flight flirting with twilight, hosting few to no inhabitants within the mountain range.

That one there? She hides in the cliff faces shadow, thousands of feet tall.

She does not receive a response *per se* but senses along the craggy terrain. Where beyond that sinkhole, she can see the mouth of the cave.

That tiny black hole?

It is said that those who dared look directly to that point-of-singularity had encountered a strange emission. And sure enough, as she looks it expands, multiplying in size until the harrowing black magnetism pulls her towards its centre. She cannot pull away. In fact, the longer she looks the wider it dilates. Quickly, she draws back, pinging back into herself, while it immediately shrinks into a dot. Feeling altered, she laughs; nervously.

Yes. I see it.

She senses their warming smiles all about her.

"No. How about, No!" she declares aloud. "No. No. NO." Shaking her head. "It's a black hole! I am Not going in there. I am not. Especially with the approach of nightfall; the atmosphere will darken in seconds." Completely dismissing her guidance.

"You are right," Alula says. "The transition leaves no margin for error if seeing day and night as separate."

Just say I could actually fly, even then, it takes a special skill to measure the accuracy needed to enter such an obscure passage. Day or night, she states matter of factly. *Anyway,* she insists, *if you put me here, in this dream, you can put me there too, no?*

"You still believe this is a dream?" They humour her.

Can you explain all this? throwing her arms through the air.

"If this is a dream then why not go for it. Jump."

And create my own nightmare? Smiling. She shakes her head. *No.*

"Are you saying once you wake from sleep your nightmares end?" Aura asks. "Day or night you'll never hide from the shadowed mind, for it will chase you, both awake and asleep, Pearl. When you come to know the undying death beneath the veils, you will no longer grasp onto the old life. It will be no longer possible to entertain that which is not true; for there is great lack in that." Aura says.

Pearl listens deeply with questioning eyes when an *aha* moment lights them up.

If I embrace that black hole, I'll be totally absorbed!

Again, their warming smiles broaden all about her.

While Pearl struggles to fathom the guidance she is given, Aura reminds her: "This portal will free you from what you are holding onto so you can fully open to the secret light that exists inside you. These veils of yours are that strong. You call it dream because you can't imagine such awakening can end your suffering and so you make do with the veils, carrying on, day by week by year, even decades. Lifetimes. Covering up. Then validate this based on what you perceive to be untouchable and unseeable but even dreams have their limits, Pearl."

Alula and Aura's whispers are flickering.

"All far-out dreams sit close inside," the Auroras hush, "the very substance of your dreams is born out of impulse of your soul's longing. This awakens the secret inside of you. You've already touched it, but your fears and nightmares keep this secret locked and firmly hidden. The only way in is to move through these veils. If you do not awaken to your secrets calling, it'll remain in the non-manifest."

Pearl listens attentively.

"Those calls unheard, and unmet, will be what destroy you. Only you can unlock your secret hidden beneath. Avail yourself to this Pearl."

You mean the secret light? If I am already that, how will I know it?

Aura consoles Pearl in the quietest of quiet whispers:

"There are times when you simply know. Other times bodily sensations, physical speakers of your truth will show you. They will guide you there. The most perceptive are goosebumps; shivers. But try not confuse those with the ones you get from Rocks, Pearl." Aura smiles kindly with sincerity. "Truth needs *no* external stimuli. The more you look inside the more you awaken to the substance of you, through feeling."

Hmm.

"Stay with us, Pearl. There are many layers, many mirrors. It's not so much a mystery for you but more that *matter* confuses and blocks your view. Your physical world validates this. Your feelings validate it. Look closely. This matter of suffering, stuck in shadows of pain echoing through life, consequently lacks great Love in you and your world. And so the hunger for it – who fills the void – reaches for quick-fix pleasures and needs. This is a poverty of the heart. It is the hardship of hunger. The problem, then, is you identify this as your reality. Life is not only about suffering, quick-fixes and compensation, Pearl. The mind, a fabrication of walls, will always be on the hunt to build more walls, enclosing spaces and forming rooms for you to compartmentalise all of life's experiences. By thinking you are one way, according to the room of emotion you're in, you limit your whole truth. Which is so much more."

Pearl, nodding her head, contemplates more deeply while the Auroras continue to impart higher purpose and meaning to lift her.

"Go beyond mind into the boundless heart of the blue sky who knows all ways. There are no doors to open in the all-expanding, endless blue space. This you have experienced already."

But still, I can't quite grasp how to get out of the mind?

"Grasping is what mind does. Sensations – speakers of truth – when used correctly become your helpers. Act on them. When you *know* in that unknown; listening and seeing via the heart, not mind, you might just get something more than mind bargained, for the heart shows a greater plan, Pearl. Trust in the mystery of this. Let go of all other matter that appears to you."

The voices envelop her in a wave.

She listens inside, and there is an echo. She notices the more intimate she becomes with that echo, whispers of love wrap around her heart. And amplify.

There is a tremor inside, I feel it, and it causes me to shiver all over with goosebumps.

As the veils start to lift, she ripples pure love into the openness of the blue.

Ah, Sky. It's blue. Everywhere.

With quiet confidence, she explores more deeply the untouched space, sinking her wide-open feeling eyes into the space of her heart. And with that, her eyes twinkle open like shiny jewels, flickering, expanding, and her skin-like dress peels off as she re-enters the gracious, naked blue…

Mmmm… I'm here!

"Tell us, how do you *feel* in this vastness of blue sky inside?" they ask, rippling back and out.

Open, free, beautiful, peaceful, the unimagined…

She excels in her newfound confidence.

"This is your truth, Pearl. You came here to elevate your self."

I did? She corrects, affirms; *Yes! I did.*

"You see what can happen when you trust in the non-manifest?"

♦

"NOW, LET'S GO back to that sinkhole."

Knowing a black mist is about to loom, the Auroras remind Pearl not to lose faith while passing through phenomena. Pearl starts sensing into the deeper knowing of all that is transient is illusion.

If it is there one minute and gone the next... it's not real, it can't be.

As though her breath is a thermal lift, she soars above rock formations, above sheer cliff tops, and above the mountain range stabbing the empty blue sky.

Wow, these cliff faces are thousands of feet high.

"Much more. It takes many lifts, Pearl, before your human eyes can even comprehend the indeterminable."

I want to accelerate more, I want to go higher.

Her flight of proximity rides along the edge of truth, pushing beyond her limits, when she is swiftly walled by confronting chunks of giant-sized cliff faces. They jut towards her, casting shadows either side of her body.

Wait, the walls, they're closing in on me.

"Weight and magnitude of towering rocks are a passing phenomena of the mind, Pearl remember; when opposites appear to intensify use this tension to move paradigm."

But the cliffs are closing in on me, either side!

Blackening, morphing into doorways and receding caves, pulling her with unbearable force. She shudders. Not realising that force is her guide, warming her directly into that.

Move out of my way. She tells the force. *Get out of my way!*

I'm trying to receive my guidance! Move, she insists, just moments before entering the magnetic field of the black hole, then contracts, completely bypassing her guidance, steering a clumsy flight, changing her course.

"What happened, Pearl?"

I can't do it. These walls are solid to me. They are real. She tuts and tantrums in the air.

No response from the Auroras but total and utter disappearance. She hears nothing. Senses nothing. As if the walls themselves have shut all out.

Yes, I know! I told you to go away! That's it. I give up. "I give up." She says aloud. "There. I said it." I am not trying anymore. A wave of relief washes over. She relaxes – while in the intensity.

And *whoosh,* the whole sky came alive with their whispers, shimmering silvery blue.

As though they'd never left!

"You've seen the moon glow in the pastel blue sky of day?"

Yes.

"Even though you know it's a phenomenon brought

about by the sun, in that moment, you don't think about the unseen great black of space that exists between sky and moon, do you? Yet you know it's there. Just because you cannot see, doesn't not mean it does not exist. It you were to start thinking or analysing, you'd lose the magic in the embrace, and the moment; gone."

Pearl contemplates.

"It is the same of the secret light. It's unimaginable. Firstly, physical matter is in the way, and secondly, well, it is the darkest black behind those walls."

Yes, but how is this relative to entering the cave at such a height?

Pearl doesn't receive the answer her mind grasps for, and never will, because no one answer ever satisfies such a mind. She must surrender.

"Jump from these illusions manifesting in the physical screens before you, all these layers of opinion and old beliefs, abandon them. Put them All to one side, just for a moment – we promise they will be there on your return; if you still want them by then." Alula and Aura smile. "You will see."

The Auroras light up the sinkhole.

She quietly sinks into the cave of her being. And with long, deep, consoling breaths she pitches her aim from high above, as an eagle pinpoints his prey, she zooms down. Her focus a growing intensity towards the deeper recesses of the mountain range.

"Now, touch the mouth of the cave with your

breath, see yourself as the breath of the cave opening."

I can't... It's opening! It's a black hole!

"Pearl, just show up." The Auroras encourage her.

Pearl pauses in the sky to correct herself: *Ok, how shall I move with you?*

"Focus on the point of singularity, be totally..."

Consumed by it. She knows what to do.

In her focus, she expands, out wide, forming her body into a wing.

"Become the wing. Angle your body in gentle turns, now close your wings. Tight."

Tight as a ball.

"Go steep and fast then, quick now, open wide, become big and long."

She opens wide. Then big and long.

"Stretch, now aim towards the centre. Yes. Gaze to the centre, on that point. Go." Alula and Aurora let her go when the subtlest billow of doubt holds her back. Her glide turns to fall. She plummets, and seconds bring her closer to the clouds below. The clouds growing, widening, bigger and greater than ever before, and just at the point of entering clouds, she swoops and gains terrific lift above. Shrouded in dismay.

It's like black ice, I can't see anything.

She thinks of what might happen, so many, hundreds of thoughts jostle with another in a nanosecond.

Pearl, she counsels herself, *this is your guidance, trust it.*

Then, she returns with a full embrace. During descent, as she passes the magnificent slate stones and cliffs, the mountainous rock forms, chunks, and shapes, there is a sudden immense G-force. She begins to shudder.

And there.

She enters the electromagnetic field of the sinkhole.

Much to Pearl's surprise, there is a complete dazzling whiteout. It carries a special eternal silence suspending time; even in high-speed motion. The next second blasts her out from that white silence into a crashing noise, charging at terminal velocity towards the sinkhole, towards its epicentre, unperturbed, like a shockwave through the elements:

I've been here before, she smiles to herself. And so do Aura and Alula.

Unstoppable, she torrents through its black vortex until blinded by pink luminosity. Pink, just pink everywhere. The pink then reduces to a delicate form and Pearl finds herself before huge slates and granite rocks. As though never airborne she stands on the base of rugged mountainous terrain. Admiring the luminous pink flower against the grey.

I can't take my eyes off your beauty; the way you glide naturally through the air out from rock.

Only she realises this evident wonder of life is trapped, suppressed, who only through will, pokes through a tiny crack. Fascinated by its yearning that feeds its crumpled roots below for preservation, she sees its outer petals fall onto the hard granite rock. Pearl shivers when an eerie wash of resemblance blows through her. She freezes in recognition of its fragile, thirst stricken lifeless stick, strangulated by other life forms. Its core dry and hungry.

I am all that flower, stuck and separate from my roots. Entrapped and entangled in past, present and future bonds, just like its roots I am bound.

"No. You are alive," the flower speaks.

I am?

"Here, there is no end, everything to lose for all to change form." Flower replies. "Please, allow me to demonstrate."

Her dying petals fall onto the rock. Every falling petal releases tears from her crying, budding center. Tears of letting go of the old, making way for reform. She then shoots up effortlessly in leaps and bounds, breathing in the sweet air. Her tears turn golden sundrops – a glimmer of hope and infinite telling. Pearl emulates her narrate glide as her fertile roots boast a flowering end. Elegantly celebrating the permanence of their essence, emitting a sweet fragrance to permeate the air.

"You see? You owe it to Her to keep living."

I do?

"She is your guide. You are Her aid. Your turnings toward Her blushing partner, of life-giving sustenance to lighter days, warms your soil that gives spark to life, flourishing and blossoming effortlessly, all from seemingly nothing, from death. You owe it to Her to keep living for all that unfurls continues to shed anew."

I can be that flower.

"I am that flower, I am alive."

Just then, the crack between the rocks widens. Pearl watches nature's force of intention and certainty unfurl. Shimmering rose petals encircle. A sudden flash rockets her back through a pink vortex and, *vroom*, swallowing her up in one gulp. Pearl vanishes into that black centre closing itself sealed.

12

THE DESCENT

*I never thought you were going to take your life
by taking mine.*

IT'S DARK.

Pearl is concussed, lying on the ground of a deep, deep-down-inside cave, beneath the highest of high mountain ranges.

A faint whisper prods her from sleep. "Pearl, wake up."

What's that? A luminous flash. Her hands scuffle her way up. *I can't move.*

Stuck in-between two giant-sized slabs, pushing and pulling.

She realises and panics: *I'm stuck. O God, I'm stuck!*

There are sharp, jagged-edged, huge rocks every-where. Surface layers of skin tear and sting and her wails echo through the mountain's inner lobes; echo with the wind. A howling vortex quakes and batters the walls from outside. She hears its spates through distant valleys.

She wiggles and twists and wiggles some more until

finally her body thrusts forth into the sombre void, loading her heavy knees onto the ground. On all fours, palming, dragging her way over crumbling stones, its surface wet and slimy. Her ankle joints fold over chunks of gravel and rocks. She looks at the final hope of light above but it's a closing glance as the whirling, black, heavy cloud stretches every direction it can. And the skylight shrinks to a pinpoint as its watchful eye closes in like a shutter, enveloping Pearl in sheer darkness.

I can't see. Anything!

She initiates movement, without physical sight of shape or form. Ground and space, vacant or not, are without trace. Her hands scan as a detector, carefully sweep and hover over bottomless black space. Moves unknowingly of what or where may materialise, plunging through dips of darkness and emptiness. Her blind investigations show the impossible avoidance of frequently jagged-edged stabs, tearing her skin. She weeps over the granite stones. She scrambles and hesitates while fine-tuning into sharp sensation of new sight, touched only by the unending and unreachable, of arriving nowhere. She stops and waits a moment. The air is stale beneath the mountain lobes. The weight is dark and pressing, her panicked lungs quake her body, even the breathing walls are not enough to pump a vacuum through her concave. Wistful, she snatches stagnant air though with great difficulty, unable to assimilate God-given gifts through her structures.

I can't breathe, I'm suffocating. Like a wilting flower.

"Then stop holding onto your breath. The space all around is weaving inside and out of you, Pearl. Remember, that space inspires."

I'm trapped inside. There is no way out.

"Let space breathe you out from within."

There's no way out, this is a nightmare!

And there she is; in great desolation. Stuck beneath the brain stem of a cold and dramatic cliff face, perpetual mourning of her future-self lingers like mouldy air. The weight of the mountain persists pressing down its walls of time. And Pearl, having anticipated nothing more but dried crusty earth and broken roots, is overwhelmed by deep, deep sadness. Her lungs spasm.

I thought I'd find my roots, my roots of the broken flower?

Once again, breath shortens, one heartbeat gone, then another, until the postponement of life immobilises her ribs and suspends her heart. Unable to breathe; the Auroras speaking through her lungs, their hushes dissolving walls that grief built inside.

Pearl, on her knees, feels her throat open and a fresh life-force pours in, bringing her to life.

"Alula? Is that you? Help me out of here!" she calls out loud in despair. "Aura, are you that mean to put me in such a tragedy, bringing me to my knees?"

"There is beauty in this depth of darkness, wherein its spaciousness; walls disappear. Do not doubt what the dark can bring. Remember us. Let the walls disappear."

Pearl reflects.

Then, slowly, reluctantly, she perseveres in motion through the moist, damp stone walls. Struggling to fathom how such findings navigated her into this point of passage squeezing her tighter, again, with nowhere to go but inward. And there! Within the mystery and wonderment of great black space, a whole new terrain appears, a new shade of sight.

Right there, in the very place she imagined her trapped roots, sits a creature. It's alive.

"What is *this*?" Pearl blurts out with disgust and utter disappointment.

Huddled in a ball. Its body is dull, a greyish-blue. Purple lines track beneath sallow patches of its skin. Pearl's stomach retches at the sight of its swollen joints, hugging emaciated limbs. She turns to soothe sore eyes but no matter where she diverts her gaze, the vision is before her, replaying murky shadows of itself anchored in potholes, dressed in mud, surrounded by puddles of tears.

It is dark, but I see so vividly.

A crescendo of primordial sounds bellows through obscure passages of the tubular cave. As information streams, the walls emulate it, and Pearl hears,

"It doesn't disguise that mud eating your brain."

Scarlett? Is that... No.

And she hears the rhythmic beat, a throbbing base-line.

What… is that, 'Noir & Haze' *I can hear?*

I've been waiting for you, to walk through my door.
I've been calling and calling your name, never once in
vain.

She shakes her head. *No. My mind is playing tricks on me.*

She starts twitching, nagging pulls feverishly attack her skin. Only a blade would relieve the insidious itchy skin that scathes.

I feel sick. She wants to propel from this forsaken trauma. *I feel splinters inside my skin, I'm sore all over.*

"I feel sick. Splinters inside my skin," the creature mimics.

"Why are you saying that, don't say that," Pearl insists out loud.

She hears the wretched voices overlapping: "Don't say that. It's sore all over," echoes throughout the walls, "splinters inside my skin."

And the throbbing baseline continues to thump throughout the walls:

I wish I could tell you someday, what I've been through.
The day my world came down on me, I've been black
and blue.

"Why are you so unfriendly? Stop it!" Pearl retorts.

"Stop it. Stop it. Stop it." Bouncing through the walls.

"I've got you, Pearl." Scarlett's voice resounds. "You violated me. You did this to me."

"Aura!" Pearl calls out. "Alula!"

Her call is of such deep longing, one her soul aches and yearns for that her consorts reappear. She feels their gentle hands cup around hers as though turning her palms to meet. On her knees, pressing palms together, dark whispers settle on her shoulders like a shawl.

"Resist nothing, Pearl, you cannot deny any one part of yourself if to feel the whole truth."

Just then, reverberations of shadows, thoughts and memories all penetrate the inner walls of the cave, they too are alive. They are a thousand feet height-and-depth tellings of time – through which she sees their light reflecting and flickering in pools of tears beside her, even in total darkness.

How strangely mesmerising, and it suddenly dawns on her, she gasps, *the secret light.*

"Listen to the waters intelligence Pearl." They hush.

The flickering vibrations inside the pools of tears are streams of information. Illuminating pools of truth as she stands barefoot and shivering before a gawping crowd inside the cave. The crowd recedes in shock at the blackened soot all over her skin. Her tears are so raw they are like blades tearing open her worn, tattered silver dress, and she has love-bite red smeared beyond her lip-line. As the dance floor continues to throb alive, FeddyB spins like a whirling Sufi. He plays, *Angel* by 'Noir & Haze.'

Someone send me an angel to watch over me,
Please send me an angel, I'm beggin' you, please.
Someone send me an angel to watch over me,
Please send me an angel, I'm down on my knees.

Held to ransom by wild eyes set in a powdery black horror she dances, spiralling, inside the beat. Dances with her shadows who tower the wall; inseparable they intertwine. They are ethereal strands in synchronistic morph, dancing through air. Shrinking from and expanding into and out of the circular crowd. And Rocks is standing at the bar, staring, while she dances as wild as the howling wind outside.

I've seen this before.

The dancing shadows join Rocks. He takes them by their arms and walks towards the exit of the Basement Club, through the black veils draping the stone archway and up the stairs to ground level, where few commuters pass. Pearl follows.

"It's that time," he tells Scarlett at the top of the stairs, "time to go home." His hair blows in a gust of wind, and Pearl, standing below, looks up through a pinhole of light.

As curiosity leads her up the stairs and levels with them both, her knees tremble, standing directly behind them. Rocks draws Scarlett closer as he snugs his arm around her waistline. Curling into each other. It's the smug smile peering over her shoulder and through those narrowing eyes that howls a wind-shear of emotion through Pearl; thrown one direction to the other, she eventually loses balance, and tips backwards.

"My dress, I... I can't move."

The stiletto heel of her shoe catches her silver dress, causing the surplus material to wrap around the heel, and she tips further from the edge of the top stair.

I'm tipping back.

On the ball of her foot, Pearl reaches out her arm, spreading her fingers as if to grasp the air.

"Rocks! I'm falling..." from his arms she falls in slow motion, but her stretched arm is far out of reach from his.

The space between herself and Rocks becomes wider and wider, too wide for his reaching arm. He cannot grasp but watch her silver dress blow in a circular swirl around her face like moving water, Pearl tips backward.

Catching a glimpse of herself in the mirror, time stops, and she floats in space.

Why am I wearing Scarlett's dress?

It's me, isn't it? The silver flashes, they are all my reflections. I'm Scarlett, it's me.

In the face of her death it's a moment of eternity as the final veil lifts from her being. Suspended in the highest elegance of exquisite free-fall, she is swathed in ghostly silk organza, just as a spider spins its web around its catch; she hangs in the air, cocooned by sheer woven silk.

"Pearl!" Rocks calls.

He stands helplessly stunned, then powerless as the sudden weight of her body drops from mid-air. The back of her head, heavy, hits every concrete step down. Thud. And the next. Thud. And the next. Thud. Thud. Thud. One by one. Blow after blow, her head knocks every step. His blood turns cold upon hearing the structural collapse of every vertebral disc shatter like the flat sound of black keyboards; tumbling on top of each other. Her neck bears all her body weight, she is concussed, lying on the ground. While the pile of notes penetrates through Rocks' nervous system, through the chilling sight and sound of life's fragility, Pearl's eyes sparkle a smile through the mirror of her imagination. That she finally sees, hidden beneath the web of illusions, the secret light of who she is. There is a sudden cessation of the wind upstairs. A deadening silence.

LOVE EVERYWHERE

*The ocean breeze shimmers up my back, settles on my
shoulders like a shawl,*

I feel you

*Through the eyes of a beggar whose home lies in the
gutter,*

I see you

A staggering drunk whose words spat at me,

I hear you

*A soft rug pulled from beneath my feet sends my world
spinning,*

I dance with you

Sweet knife of betrayal who cut my heart,

I am you.

13

SILVER TRAILS & CHASING
SHADOWS

The trees stand
happy in the breeze.

PEARL, HELD IN a loving embrace, gently rocks in the sky through invisible cradles and caress above Moon Mirror. She listens to the Auroras consolations.

"We tried reaching you many times through the elements, Pearl. You kept shunning us, all the time running away from yourself in fact. All you were interested in was chasing your shadow. You even said it yourself."

Hearing her echoes in the distance. *Is my shadow chasing me or am I chasing my shadow?*

"You sat alone in the Antenna Rooms that night, even spoke to your future shadow-self whom you named Scarlett. You watched as she lived her parallel life in the wing mirror of the car. She is too destructive to care. Eventually, we got your attention through silver flashes. It was when you finally hit rock bottom, where you *had* to let go, that you noticed our brightness. Letting go is no simple feat, Pearl, it's a constant effort because of the grieving process that takes place, but it's a powerful lesson of detachment.

We carried you through the Earth's atmosphere where your darker recesses of the psyche naturally attuned with the subtlest of sound to purify your shadows and veils. We navigated your course specifically to a special mountain range of the Himalaya, Mehru, representing the subconscious part of your planet's brain. Here is where we uplifted you beyond the transpersonal. That by way of deep purification through neural pathways of the mountains lobes we revealed your darkness for a luminosity to stream in; flooding the unconscious with light. The darker it appears the brighter the light in its contrast. Destruction is sometimes needed to make way for new, Pearl, you had to suffer the violence and pain of the elements. The glimpses we imparted kept you going whilst enduring the harsh elements. That by taking you into the darkest depths of the Earth's core through a sinkhole – the heart of the mountain – we not only transmitted your nerve impulses, but also transmuted all your suffering and fears into Love. Pearl, you wanted to go there. The two reasons you desired to reach us are one, to embrace and overcome the three levels of human pain, physical, emotional and mental."

And to escape my sabotage patterns?

"No. That's a consequence of neglecting pain, although woke you to the second and more penetrative, which is your deep-calling from within. Your truth. This is your longing, Pearl. Your misinterpretation of this longing had been largely misguided by mind-altering substances giving so-called out-of-body mystical experiences. You even confessed your intuitions in a conversation with Pop because deep in the core of your being you know, you know your truth. That life couldn't possibly be so cruel to be *only* about a body of pain and hunger."

I did? She smiles, then confesses, *I admit, it's true. I knew my truth was pulling and tugging on me, deep down inside I knew.*

"In your agony, your limp body lay shattered, while passing, you left behind a lifeless, crumpled shell. That pain you felt in a delicate sprawl lit your silent-scream of embers on fire."

I saw a peaceful silvery cloud in that moment, just one, it ambled across my face and I saw myself, I mean, I saw pure spirit.

"Your shadows evaporated, Pearl. Only, when you finally let go, your soul departed too."

◆

ROCKS BOLTED DOWN the stairs to Pearl whose crumpled shell lay pristinely, with so much fragility, and though perishable, a luminescence glowed around her body.

"Pearl, wake up," he wept in her ear. And then he heard the intrusive sound of sirens. As they neared he collected himself together. "I gotta go. I've got to go." He took the pink rose from his pocket she had given him moments before at the bar, and placed a petal over each eye, kissing her lips. "I'm sorry," he sobbed, then disappeared in a flash. This time, he really left her for dead.

◆

"HE CHOSE TO run, out of his own fears," the Auroras continue. "Of course, he doesn't see it as choice because he too is bound in it. But he never gave up on you, Pearl. The only language of love he understands is in deals and favours, though he did beguile you. Such a love keeps him in the dark. Rocks is the kind who drifts on one wave of thought throughout an entire ocean of life. He swims with the current and not against it, always taking him back to where he started. He can't help but rewrite his same errors, unless opening to those glimpsing mysteries in-between dual worlds where pure love exists, eternally waiting for him – to see, to hear, to grow to feel to expand. Those openings are the pouring of grace. But there he will remain until a flame in the air unearths and wakes him out of suffering. And you, Pearl, dived from the cloud of thought into an infinite ocean of air. For this is your longing. Not only moving as the ocean does but absorbing your dreams and fears into the unseen, into the unknown. This kind of trust brings so much power. For waking out of sleeping shadows beneath the seabed released you into the expansive ocean of consciousness – for every unfolding wave, you swam against its current. And through that fierceness, transmuted your shadows into light. You see, the extreme of opposites brings a balance of a new one; the two melding together forging a third. That trust in fear, once able to let go, turning all limitations into a power surge, is what lifted you out. We held and carried you until you were ready to leap from sea into air where you finally slipped in-between the two worlds."

I am eternally grateful that you hauled me from this deep sleep.

"Do you remember we gave you opportunity to return to Earth by a great push through the ionosphere?"

Pearl nods.

"That push gave a breath of life back into your Earth body, but you resisted even this because you wanted to go further, you wanted *to know.* Tired and disappointed of the basic conditional and unrequited versions of human love, you transferred all your love to journey with us into freedom. That by digging deep into unworthiness, of all imperfections and flaws in exchange for truth, for this, you called on us for help. Pulling yourself from rock bottom up is your story, Pearl, from where you gravitated mind into heart, transferring all into love through will, yours and ours," Aura smiled a warm embrace.

◆

"NOW YOU HAVE arrived in-between two worlds you must choose your new form. Pearl, do you stay or return to Earth?"

Back? To Earth?

"When you wake back into your Earth body this *will* be like dream, but no ordinary dream, for you will be ever touched by embodiment of truth and new sight." The Auroras are dancing around her.

"But first, we celebrate! We have some flying to do, come on, we can't be late for the party!"

Party?

"Yes, Pearl, party is play. And play is essential. It is where the real magic happens." The Auroras smile.

Just then a giant bulbous cloud ambles by, towering up and down, building itself a city of cloud. She flies though skyscrapers of clouds and labyrinths of flight paths, and magnificent formations encircle her. Tip-toeing cloud to cloud, her eyes sparkle in delight by the silvery rain that traverses before her. With the orange sun behind, the raindrops shimmer like light screen-dividers of crystal beaded curtains, sparkling the whole sky silver. It is a shower of grace.

3

14

METAMORPHOSIS

Nature's subtle dance,
it's so still here,
the flowers breathe…
It's so still.

STRONG, UPPER WINDS aerate the sky, clearing and revealing a hot blue, moving the shadows of clouds – quickly, across the mountains terrain. Pearl's elegant tiptoe landing impresses a great boulder sitting on the base of its mountain plateau. The boulder smiles. Beside the cave's mouth are pink rose petals complimenting the fresh earth. Pearl breathes her vibrant scent, rich and potent. She lifts her labradorite-like, magnetic eyes towards the sun.

She is surrounded by fresh fir forests of the mountain's granite heights. The silent forest speaks, bringing forth spirit within. Trees and ferns are overgrown, their very indulgence sinking into themselves, is where pure love emerges. Such a love cannot help but branch out and permeate healing and compassion through their friendly arms.

What is that sound? She is listening to heartbeats, *lots of them inside of me.*

She pauses – hypnotic birdsongs lace the naked blue sky, she floats on their echoes, and the peacocks calls, rising above the mountaintops.

This place, it's magical.

There are motionless rivers of cloud sitting in between mountain walls, spilling over clifftops like waterfalls, flowing through the valleys.

Trickling inside of me.

Its gush, a spring of meaning and Love, pours inside and out through her dewy, radiant, glowing skin. The more transparency reveals itself, the more porous she becomes. There is no hiding. She is completely bare, naked with nature.

The air is charmed by the Auroras' smiles. "What do you see, Pearl?"

I can't seem to find the words to explain, I…

She gasps, watching ripples of energy penetrate beyond her physical outline.

Did you see that? My body is merging with nature, it's more than seeing. I feel, then become. The thread of life, it's weaving through me and, though time elapses, I am awake, I'm awake to every heartbeat of nature as it tremors and wavers throughout me.

Nature's movie unfolds before her, behind, both sides, above and below. Multiplying doorways of varying landscapes dissolve and evolve. Door after door after door, enveloping in and out of fractal worlds, screens of transparency, illuminating like heartbeats. Pearl merges one form to the next. Nature cannot wait for its natural process for its sudden need to burst into life override its natural laws, eclipsing time. Sunsets rise and fall simultaneously. Flowers blow in the gentle wind like flowing skirts, their petals lift and take to the air as wings by the slightest breeze and transform into butterflies. Pearl barrel-spins alongside them, fluttering towards the West as the sun rolls boldly down triangular mounds, spraying orange misty veils over luscious green terrains. Wherever and whatever Pearl sets sight on, sporadic fragments of life flourish there on instant reflection. There are foxgloves, boasting their buds like dazzling jewels, hanging from wild ferns trellising up and down the mountain's edge before blossoming into fuchsia-bells. Colours gloat brightly. Columns of giant-sized grass blades point twelve meters high toward the sky and race their way up alongside purple lupins through tumbling waterfalls. They become an emergence of crystal shards. And nearby there sits an azure blue millpond. The suns reflection floats in its centre and dilates the fluid surface – blushing to its partner above.

Sleeping swans glide on the gentle ripples and keep their eye on Pearl while she balances elegantly in the shallow water beside pink flamingos. And there, beneath the palms, they retreat coolly in the shade. Ulysses butterflies are playing in flight among the smudge of pink. Pearl leaps into the air, ecstatic, fluttering as metallic-blue emperor wings.

After play she lands, swims alongside the swans to the water's edge and arrives on a soft carpet of bronze and copper mulch. Kissing the earth in exaltation, she comes nose to nose with dragonflies, who pat her dry with their helicopter wings. She kneels over a giant, shiny, black rock. The reflection of its brilliance glosses over grass-green blades, where millions of dewdrops glitter their tips like diamond-clusters, and sparkle the day-night glow. Pearl glides with astonished eyes at the flourishing orgy of buttercups peppering the wild grass. The upside of their petals projecting holograms of light, bouncing in every direction. Onto golden-reeds where shafts of amber-light poke through and stroke the heather, striking a purple-haze to wobble up and down the vivid-green breathing hills. And onto land, the ground a patchwork of water-filled cushions of grass, resembling tiny miniature shaped fern-trees and micro-stars. The cosmic grass twinkles between her toes. And utter wonderment leads her into deep, expansive awareness.

I've never felt such transparency and oneness with nature. Such aliveness.

Her eyes are a circle of smiles when an epiphany of fireworks shivers from her consciousness.

"You don't have to become a flower. You are a flower." She hears. "It was you who burst into life's existence.

It's always here and in you. You are everything a plant and insect and every human feels, as they do you. You are inside them as they are you. Everything you see is in you, always has and will be. Should you turn from such, you turn away from that part of you." The Auroras' hushes are a thousand lullabies.

"To see in-between the light and shadows is to be in the space between thoughts, wherein that vastness exits the non-manifest of infinite possibilities waiting to be lived. The ineffable, waiting to be seen."

Surrounded by majestic mountains, what could be so perfectly mesmerising as to enter the azure-blue millpond and merge with a hundred-thousand prism of herself. The transparency and becoming of who she is. Of the secret light now revealed; Her innate power.

Floating, face up. The universe sparkling inside, behind her blissful eyes. The rose-gold aura of moon set in midnight blue shines brightly as she hears the omnipresence of her consoles. Honouring her destiny they ask,

"Pearl… what did you decide?"

Her eyes are floating. A background noise – beep, beep, beep – wakes her from deep rest.

WHAT IS THAT noise and that yucky, disinfectant smell?

Waking fully into her Earth-body she sees a blurry white vision form into a human, blinks her eyes open and closed a few times and is greeted by a doctor.

"Ah. Hello, young lady. Or should I say, lucky lady." He smiles, taking her pulse. "I don't suppose you remember anything?" He lifts his stethoscope to his ears.

"Um…" She takes time to reply – it's been a while since she last saw another human, never mind communicated with one. "I don't think you'd believe me." She smiles. Remembering everything.

"I doubt that very much. You've been on a journey."

She had been in a coma.

"How long…?"

"A few days."

"Only? Gosh. Am I… okay… do I have everything?"

"Given the fall you had, you'll be relieved to hear, just a few bruises."

"That's it?"

"I need you to stay a few more days for tests and monitoring. All being well, then you'll be free to go. As I said, you are a lucky lady."

He hesitates.

"Go on," she says, knowing there is more.

"There is something else, Pearl. I'm curious about the deep fissures on both palms and knees."

Pearl listens.

"Those wounds, evidently from rocks or stones, were not at all like those from a fall down the stairs. They were quite severe. Deep cuts and ruptures."

"Were?"

"Yes. The thing is, Pearl, they sealed up the next day,

leaving old scars. I have to say, Pearl, in all the twenty years of my medical profession I have never seen such a thing. Is there anything you remember at all, before the fall perhaps?"

She remembers the Auroras' whispers; that she would wake from no ordinary dream. She smiles at the phenomena. "No, Doctor."

"Very well. That will do for now. Meanwhile I bid you rest. Do you think you can do that?"

"Yes, Doctor." She smiles. He leaves the room, and his nurse follows.

Pearl lies on the bed in a soft, dreamy calm, though with an immense impulse to see Rocks. She knows the right time will present itself; meanwhile, she is content to lie on that hospital bed, ever so patient, ever so calm.

Rocks did not seek any form of enquiry about Pearl at all. He didn't go to the hospital after her fall to see if she survived or not. To see if she was okay. If she needed help. He didn't once visit. He didn't care. He who left her for dead.

◆

A few months later…

PEARL ADJUSTS TO a new body and new life. She is packing up her London home, knowing her time with Rocks would come.

That time is now.

Rocks is walking through the early evening back streets of Soho when his phone beeps. He turns a corner, lifting his phone from his back pocket, and opens the text while walking.

He semi-recognises the number. Frowns to think. Then stops. A chill blows through him as he just happens to be standing outside The Basement Club. He shivers. "Na," he thinks aloud. "That's not Pearl's number." He mutters, "It can't be."

He opens the text and sure enough, it's Pearl.

Hey Rocks. Meet me where you like your drink – tomorrow 10 a.m. Xx

She'd always went there for him, it's the only café that serves alcohol at that time.

He stands numb, in shock, as if the wind wipes him of all life-force. His face turns white.

He has to see her. He can't not.

And she knows he won't be able to help himself; he doesn't have it in him to resist.

TOMORROW ARRIVES ONLY too soon for Rocks yet he arrives early. He goes inside the Corner Cafe, in Soho. He orders a pot of tea for two.

"Make it a builders. Oh an' a pot of hot water, mate," he adds, remembering she likes to top up her tea, scorching hot. "And honey."

He takes a seat right down the other end, at the back of the café, so he can watch Pearl's entrance from a distance. He's nervous. Waves of nausea wash over him. His mind performs gymnastics: what does she want, what will she say, is this a trap.

The waitress places a tray on the table: a pot of tea. A stainless steel pot, full of boiling-hot water. Honey, milk, two cups and saucers. "Get me a whisky shot, will ya."

SUDDENLY, AS IF appearing from thin air, Pearl is standing there, right before him. He jumps – where did she come from, he thinks. He didn't see her enter the café. He didn't see her make way over to the table. She just appeared. His hands are trembling, he doesn't understand himself – nausea, shakes, foggy vision – and he knocks the teacup and saucer in a fumble, and the pot of boiling hot water. It spills over the table and pours over onto his lap.

"Shit." He stands up, impulsively rubs his jeans. "Argh. Should 'ave got a mug," he laughs nervously, aware of his awkwardness, and that she hadn't bothered to fuss over him. She always did fuss over him. He notices how steep her beauty is, standing high in a beautiful, dewy, moonlike glow. And her cheeks, soft rose. He is in utter disbelief that she is alive, and in utter awe, stunned by her striking aura that is full of warmth.

The waitress returns. He knocks back the whisky.

"Sit down won't ya," he tells her.

She sits opposite and all she does is look at him. Her soft stares penetrating firmly, draws his avoiding eyes to hers.

He tries his toughest to be tough. "You look clean. Wonder 'ow long you'll last."

She no longer relates to his language, says nothing, but smiles, her soft yet penetrative stares squashing him back into his squalor.

"You know where to find me when ya need it, y'kno'."

But she has all of the mountain presence about her, and he cannot hide from himself, never mind Pearl. It's in his eyes. The sudden cast of remorse, sorrow, regret, drenched by her pools of truth. The mountain emanates from her, and as harrowing as those cliff faces were that once closed in on her, now close in and press on him.

She returns his looks into her stony-turned eyes, where there is nothing but softness and compassion – but this he does not see what he can see. He cannot move through the embodiment of her mountain psyche that is crushing him, squashing and flattening the power he once had over her. And there is an agonising pain, crushing, pressing on his chest. He cannot breathe. His veins are bulging from his throat and face.

"What's happening? I can't breathe, help me, Pearl, help me."

She turns and walks away, to leave him in his pitiful, diminishing state.

ROCKS' NOT MET by mere revenge. That would be futile. No, Pearl knows he too must undergo his own suffering and reform, if he wants, and so prays deeply for his purification, for his soul, and for all those who had been in his hands. And she means it. With all her mountain power, and he feels it.

Stepping outside the café, she breathes in the air. Nourished by a warming breeze she looks up and expands with the Auroras glowing beyond the silvery veils where she sees through the greatest lie of the sky.

A message

If Pearl speaks to you and you long to reawaken and be touched by the wisdom of your heart, connect with someone who knows. Find out more info@ niamhdolores.com

Note on the author

Niamh's journey revealed a surrender to the heart through which she looks no further than to deepen the experience of the true self. When not guiding, planting, or writing, Niamh frequents to wide-open spaces, the sea, the sky... and marvels at life's great mystery.

Lightning Source UK Ltd.
Milton Keynes UK
UKHW011848070922
408502UK00001B/53